virtually

IMPOSSIBLE

HIGH-TECH CRIME SOLVERS

virtually

IMPOSSIBLE

BARBARA EBEL, M.D.

HIGH-TECH CRIME SOLVERS

Copyright © 2020 by Barbara Ebel, M.D.

Paperback ISBN-13: 978-1-7324466-9-4
ebook ISBN-13: 978-1-7324466-8-7

This book is a work of fiction. Names, characters, places and events are the product of the author's imagination or are used fictitiously. Any resemblance to actual events, persons, or locations is coincidental.

CHAPTER 1

Although he was not waiting on the birth of a baby, Hook Hookie paced with a slight limp up and down the aisle of the lab like an expectant father. He always figured a code was embedded in his genes to not sit still for long periods of time, and if anyone should know about genes, it was him.

The rubber mat between the two counters showed wear and tear where the genetic M.D. scientist traversed back and forth. It was a redundant part of his day—waiting for one or both of the centrifuge machines to stop spinning—so pacing, and deep thinking, kept him occupied.

Two different sized centrifuges stood on both flat working spaces next to him as the dull whirling noise sounded from the one on the higher speed. Lab vials were placed inside the machines all day long, allowing centrifugal force to separate their contents because of the different density of the samples' substances. The machines were also used to remove moisture, so that the samples could be refined down to their denser, pure form.

The lab door opened, and Freddie Simpson entered. As one of the medical campus's security guards, he occasionally paid Hook a visit. He was a retired cop earning a pension, and now enjoying a slower pace and a little spending money on the side because of his job in 'retirement.'

Hook came to a halt for Freddie. The retired cop often had questions about the work done in the laboratory, and seemed enamored by Hook's credentials—M.D., FCAP, Ph.D., and/or Molecular Genetic Pathologist. And those were just his academic credentials, known by many at Monument Medical Center in Atlanta, Georgia where he worked. A signature line on one of Hook's letters would need three lines if he included his Air Force titles.

"Just passing by," Freddie said. "How are you doing today, Dr. Hookie?"

"Not bad. How about yourself?" Hook expected the same old answer, just like the way the man wore his uniform shirt every day—wrinkled and a bit too big.

"Unlike some, I'm fortunate to be alive and kicking."

1

"Keep it up," Hook responded.

Freddie patted his faint gray mustache and nodded. At the doorway, he turned around. "Dr. Hookie, be extra careful to lock up the lab tonight when y'all leave. Regardless of whether someone misplaced a piece of equipment in another department, or it was stolen, they can't find it."

"Sure thing," Hook said. The timer sounded on a centrifuge, so he went to the machine and carefully removed each vial.

"Hook" was not Dr. Hookie's real first name. His nickname was plucked from his last name forty-seven years ago by his Air Force buddies in Vietnam, and those guys were experts at cannibalizing each other's names. Most of the guys in his squadron went over there with one name, and came back with another.

His real first name was "Richard," but since the early seventies, rarely did anyone call him that. On applications and formal paperwork, he was careful to write down his birth name. However, even on his Air Force pension documents, he had managed to sneak in Richard (Hook) Hookie.

Hook tinkered on with his samples and strolled with his droopy gait back to his desk, which at least was housed in a small office in the rear corner of the lab. He stood by the window, but looked to the left wall, where three shelves kept the pictures and degrees he wanted in his close quarters.

Hook was always interested in biology, even while he attended the Air Force Academy. Returning to the states after serving in Vietnam, he never thought that subject would lay the groundwork for his future studies. Avoiding any PTSD, he plunged into academics and earned his M.D. and PhD. His primary thesis involved human genetics and, since then, he not only held his current prestigious position, but he was a sought-after consultant for major criminal investigations by police departments and organizations up to, and including, Homeland Security. He qualified as a person with an unconventional career path!

"Who woulda thought?" Hook mumbled, scanning the shelves at the pictures and degrees which lay testimony to his past. Sometimes he pressed on, so immersed in his work, that he forgot to allow himself a pat on the back for all his accomplishments. Not many people could claim his type of background at seventy-three years old. Nor had he hung up the reins yet. No way, he thought. He wanted to be working up until the day they dropped his ashes, or his box, underneath Mother Earth.

After straightening the two airplane models on the windowsill and a few piles on his desk, Hook grabbed his light jacket from the coat stand. Remembering what Freddie had mentioned, he locked his office door behind him, which he didn't always do since the lab would also be locked up.

He poked his head into the last two aisles on his way out and said goodnight to Cynthia and Alex, two workers in his lab. "Last one out, lock up," he said.

"Sure thing, Dr. Hookie," Alex said.

He could count on them. Alex would be sure to follow him out soon because his evening gym time was punctual.

Although he knew exactly where to find his black Jeep, Hook needed to weave through the parking lot of the multi-building complex like walking in a maze. He unbuttoned his jacket. It was April, but in Georgia that meant the temperature could swing forty degrees from sunrise to early afternoon. He clicked his key fob, slid into his vehicle, and rolled down his window.

As he stopped at the first stop sign out of the lot, a physician he knew stepped off the curb and advanced to his window. "Not going to the monthly medical staff meeting?"

"I'm giving myself a pass. I'm chief cook and bottle washer at home tonight."

"But you always are."

"So true. Take notes for me."

The doctor laughed, shook his head no, and said good night with a pat on the window sill.

Hook eased forward, aware of a few more white-coated physicians headed into the main hospital. None of them would be working over in their offices tonight.

He glanced in the rear view mirror and caught the baldness on the top of his head. Although it made a complete perfect circle, he pulled back the silvery hair which still grew from the sides and the back, banded into a ponytail. Sometimes he wondered if he looked more like a left-over hippie from Woodstock rather than someone retired from the Air Force.

In a few minutes, he streamed classic rock music on the radio and headed northeast to a classic, charming subdivision seeded with couples and kids of every age. He liked the diversity, and his wife, Susan, liked the neighbors. When he pulled into the garage and shut the engine, he carefully slid out. He favored his right leg, a limp he carried as a 'scar,' from Vietnam. But he didn't acquire it from being wounded in action, rather he was injured from roughhousing in the officer's club.

Sometimes it amazed Hook how a small segment of his entire seventy-three years could leave such a lasting imprint. He couldn't remember much of the food he and his squadron were served in the officer's club in Vietnam, but what he did come home with was a true love for Thai food—mostly because of the Thai restaurant on the base, where he had eaten dinner as much as possible. That fact, besides him being the usual cook at home, caused him to regularly whip up Thai recipes which tasted far better than most of the same ethnic food served in regional restaurants.

With a few harsh clangs, he pulled out a pot and two frying pans and set them on the stove. After putting pad Thai noodles in the pot to boil, he assembled chopped shallots, garlic, and ginger, and soon made them golden brown in heated peanut oil. At the same time, he prepped thin slices of chicken and seared them in hot oil.

"Don't make it too spicy," he heard over the buzz of the overhead stove fan. Having gotten up from her recliner, his wife Susan grabbed a diet soda from the refrigerator, and glanced at his food assembly line.

"Don't worry, dear. I never do. I can garnish my serving with a little chili garlic sauce."

"Thank you." She poured her soda into a glass and peeled away without offering to help. Opening the door to the deck, she exited with a book, while their cat, Bentley, took the opportunity to slink out as well.

Hook frowned after her. With all Susan's medical problems, he couldn't fathom why she drank diet soda—devoid of any nutrition. He drank his favorite soda as well, but without artificial sweetener, and kept

4

protein drinks in the closet which she didn't touch.

He turned back to draining the noodles, added eggs to his shallot mixture, and soon mixed the entire concoction with pad Thai sauce and chicken. Adding bean sprouts, lime, and crushed roasted peanuts, he was ready to eat. The smell he'd created in the entire kitchen was driving his taste buds crazy.

He opened the door to the deck. "Wanna eat?" he asked Susan.

"Would love to."

"I hope so. I skipped a monthly medical staff meeting to come home and whip this up. Not that I'm complaining, because I didn't want to sit through it."

"Sometimes I benefit from your intolerance of conferences and business meetings."

He ladled her a serving on a plate. "Smart medical conferences are up my alley, or in-depth investigative meetings where we're trying to solve something, but business meetings that go on and on..." He left his words hanging in the air.

Susan took her plate from him and nodded. "Unfortunately, I'm your sounding board when you come home from one. If anyone understands you, it's me."

"Thanks, honey. Now let's follow Bentley to the dinner table and enjoy the food."

Like marriage vows, for better or for worse, Monument Medical Center had so many medical buildings connected together that a person could avoid breathing fresh air all day and walk one causeway or connector from one end of the campus to the next. In Hook's opinion, connecting the hospital, the doctor's office building, the medical school, the school's departments, the outpatient clinic, cancer center, and various labs was a good idea only insofar as transporting patients in wheelchairs or stretchers, or on bad weather days when folks didn't need to go outside.

Other than that, engineers and architects had done a fine job in keeping human beings glued to the gloomy inside with blaring fluorescent lights. And he should know since lab time dominated most of his days. He loved his work too much, otherwise he would be working nine-to-five in the great outdoors.

The next day, he sat in the "Campus Coffee and Bakery Shop" smack between the hospital and doctor's office building. More vibrant and less generic than the hospital cafeteria, almost every morning he savored a dark roast while eating a fresh toasted bagel.

Hook peeled back a packet of apricot jam and slathered it on his bagel. Walking around the corner were his two lab employees, Cynthia and Alex.

"Uh, oh," Hook said. "You two coming into work together? Does that mean you're sleeping together?"

Cynthia's eyes grew wider than normal. "Dr. Hookie!"

"What? I wasn't born yesterday. Co-workers sleeping together is a stupid idea. Just remember that I told you so."

Alex looked down, avoiding the issue.

"Go buy something," he instructed them. "Sit down with me before we head to the lab."

A few more sips of coffee and the two younger lab rats joined him. They ate in silence as Hook intermittently scrutinized the bundle of pink hair which appeared overnight on one side of Cynthia's head.

"It's a hairpiece, Dr. Hookie," she said.

"I like it. A lot more colorful than my dismal ponytail."

Slipping in from the hallway, Freddie Simpson sauntered in and stood next to their table, behind two other customers. He put his hands near his hips, jostled his belt, and nodded at them.

Hook understood body language like his Vietnam days had depended on it. "Morning Freddie. Is there some excitement on your job already this morning?"

"You bet. Dr. Putnam's practice manager just called me when they opened up his office. His EKG machine is missing, as if it vanished into the clouds." He furrowed his brow at Hook. "Hey, you used to fly planes, maybe you can track down, or track up, his piece of equipment."

"Very funny, Freddie. Stick a little genetics investigation in there, and maybe I can help you out."

"Nah, that won't be needed. Somebody probably stuck the damn thing into the closet while they were pulling out their coat to go home last night. I'll look into this."

"That's why they pay you the big bucks." Finished with his bagel, Hook rose from the table, and waved his hand at Alex and Cynthia. "Let's get to work."

Freddie patted the hair growth on his upper lip and ordered a cup of espresso to-go.

CHAPTER 2

Freddie strolled through the connecting hallway to the physicians' tall office building and occasionally sipped his espresso. He pressed the button in the elevator for the fifth floor, and soon headed behind the front desk of the old practitioner's OB/GYN office.

"You must be security," Dr. Putnam said as he lingered with a chart in his hands. For five years, the man kept stretching out his plans for retirement, and as the months ticked by, his scoliosis became more noticeable, and the pattern of the suspenders he wore became bolder.

"Security is my middle name, but Freddie Simpson's my real name. An EKG machine turned up missing?" Freddie gawked at the bright bands supporting the man's trousers which peeked out from his white coat.

The physician placed the chart back in the rack. "I'm Dr. Putnam. Follow me." Down the hall, he let Freddie enter a bright room with medical equipment and supplies. "This corner space is where we keep the machine. See, it's gone, but it was here yesterday."

"I thought only cardiologists and primary care doctors read EKGs, not doctors delivering babies."

"My partner is double boarded in OB/GYN and internal medicine. He wanted the ability to run EKGs when he started working here. It was a smart decision." He stared at the empty space, wanting the machine to reappear like magic.

Freddie lowered his Styrofoam cup on a shelf and narrowed his eyes. "Any change in routine yesterday when you closed the office?"

"My partner and I went to the medical staff meeting in the hospital. On those nights, we let our staff leave a little early as well. We all trotted out of here like we were in a 4th of July parade."

"After which, so to speak, the fireworks happened in this room. Who's the person who runs the machine?"

"A multi-talented nurse named Cora Bell."

"Mind if I talk to her, or other staff, so I don't take up more of your time?"

"Yes, do what you must. Check back with me before you leave."

Freddie grabbed his Styrofoam cup, the men split up, and the security guard soon was talking to a slight woman wearing purple from the headband in her hair to her dark trousers. He suspected her shoes, which he couldn't see, were purple too.

"Want me to top off that coffee you're holding?" Cora asked him, poised in the kitchenette with a full pot in her hand.

"Regular coffee? Sure thing. That'll soften the blow after the espresso I just drank."

She poured while Freddie held his cup steady.

"Don't take this the wrong way," Freddie said and laughed, "but you didn't desire an EKG machine at your house, did you?"

"Nope, after I leave here each day, I want nothing more than to ditch my job in the after hours."

"As far as you know, you were the last one to use it?"

"Yes, and only one patient all day yesterday needed an EKG and it was in the late afternoon. I ran the tracing, put the tracing in her chart, and returned the machine to the back room."

"That door stays unlocked?"

"Yes, the only door that gets locked at the end of the day is the main one to the hallway. I think Dr. Putnam locked it. We all filed out within minutes of each other."

Freddie held his coffee, too hot to drink. "Appreciate it. Any other substantial piece of equipment ever go missing before?"

"Not that I'm aware of."

"Thanks for your time. And for the java."

"My pleasure."

Freddie signaled Dr. Putnam in the hallway as he stepped out of a patient's room. "I'm going to check the door lock for evidence of any tampering. However, I'm not coming up with anything suspicious or harmful to your practice except for the one missing article. Do you want me to pursue this any further? Report it to the police? And will you file an insurance claim?"

Dr. Putnam hooked his finger into a suspender and grimaced. He gave it serious thought. "Probably not worth the trouble. I think we can afford a new one; maybe it's a blessing in disguise. Although damn if I know where the machine went."

Freddie nodded. "Call me back if anything else comes to mind." He stopped at the entrance and, using his keen previous knowledge, he scrutinized the keyhole to the door. There was no evidence of tampering to the lock. He shrugged his shoulders, went down to the first floor central lobby, and assumed his favorite alert posture. There was nothing like extending his career in a scaled-down version of his life's work.

Hook dodged from one lab aisle to the next all morning, multitasking more than usual. His mouth became dry, and he realized he could use something to drink, so he grabbed a sip of bottled water in his office. Glancing at his desk calendar, he was reminded of a promise he'd made to be at the cancer center in a few minutes.

Slipping on his white jacket, Hook alerted Cynthia and Alex of his departure. "I'm headed to the cancer center," he said, "to fill in for the genetic counselor because she has another work commitment."

Alex stood against the counter, his hands holding the edge of the upper shelf, while he flexed his biceps. "Have fun. See you after lunch."

"Do some isotonic contractions for me. I'm not taking growth hormones and when you end up being my age, muscles turn into limp oatmeal in a bowl."

"I'll remember that, Dr. Hookie."

"Me too," Cynthia chimed in, peering through a microscope.

Downstairs, Hook avoided walking through the maze of ground-floor corridors, and stepped outside. Despite his limp, he half darted across the common area where several pieces of architecture and a fountain dotted the square.

The cancer center hailed as the newest building in the medical center. Even the appeal it had to patients was stellar. While patients received their chemotherapy drips in the infusion room, they could stare out at a garden and a soothing mural. Next to three benches, the volunteers maintained rose bushes, marigolds, and a goldfish pond.

More importantly, Hook believed the nurses in the cancer center were far superior to the hospital's. Rarely was human error a problem in treating the fragile and sickly patients who came in regularly for their nasty cancer appointments.

Hook opened the door to a genetic counselor's room, an office which he used quite often as well. He was overly qualified but, when necessary, he filled in for Anita's patients' appointments. He glanced at the pictures of her family members next to the computer, and opened the envelope she had left for him.

The phone buzzed from the lobby's front desk, so Hook answered.

"Dr Hookie," the receptionist said, "I saw you sneak in there. Mrs. Larson, the eleven-thirty appointment is here."

"I'll be right out."

Through the automatic doors, Hook strolled into the spacious, comfortable lobby where a room went deep down the left with chairs, a large screen TV, a coffee and snack set-up, and even a round table with shelves of boxed games. He glanced around, and spoke aloud. "Karissa Larson?"

A woman with soft features popped up from a nearby chair and matched his medium height. Hook extended his hand. "I'm Dr. Hookie, considered around here to be mostly a part-time genetic counselor. I'm more of what you'd call a lab rat and a sometimes part-time asset to law enforcement."

"You sound like one of those people who become bored doing one thing."

"Guilty as charged."

Maneuvering back to the office, he stayed beside her. She wore a pink cap, a color chosen by many breast cancer patients, and no hair weaved its way down alongside her ears or neck. The hat stylishly hid her chemotherapy side effect of baldness.

Hook pointed straight to one of the cushy chairs in front of the desk. "Can I fetch you something to drink?" he asked.

"No, I'm good. One of my jobs is to stay well hydrated. The GI effects of my treatments demand it. Vomiting and diarrhea from chemo are not 'side effects,' they can be 'deadly side effects.' I already landed in the hospital once, and I was so far behind in fluids, that my blood pressure stalled at a mere eighty over forty."

"I am a physician, so I sympathize with your plight. What you are going through is not easy."

Her courageous smile faded and she tilted her head. "An M.D. too? Are there other credentials you keep hidden?"

"Retired Colonel from the Air Force. Forget about me. What is your background, if I may ask?"

She chuckled first. "A past Colonel wearing a ponytail. I love it. Me? I worked as a head nurse running the schedule in this hospital's OR, and I only 'retired' last year. Breast cancer was my reward for doing so. Fate has destined me to not scratch off items on my travel bucket list."

"I'm sorry to hear it," he said sincerely, glancing down at the sheet to note her age of sixty-six. "This will be behind you before you know it and then it will all seem like a bad dream."

"Thank you. I hope you are correct."

Comfortable with her and her background, Hook nodded. She would probably grasp much of what they would discuss.

"Looking at your information, the pathology of your breast biopsies puts you at a clinical prognostic stage group of 1B and you were positive for all three prognostic markers—receptor positive for ER antigen, PgR antigen, and HER-2. So that means you must be getting chemotherapy as well as monoclonal antibodies because you were receptor positive."

"Yes, lucky me. The only thing going for me is that my lymph nodes may not be positive, but the surgeon said we won't know for sure until I go for surgery."

"Which brings us to why this genetic testing we're about to do is going to help you out. Have you made arrangements for surgery yet?"

"Yes. We've scheduled a mastectomy in three weeks. In the meantime, there are no treatments, so that I can build myself up a little before it."

"Good. Here's the thing. We will test you, to determine if hereditary causes contributed to your cancer. If genetics play a role, it is possible your chances of a second breast cancer are much higher than the general population."

"In which case I can consider him doing a second breast mastectomy at the same time."

"Correct. You have a significant multi-lobular cancer. Were you getting routine mammograms?"

"Yes, like clock work. This thing took off like an invasive weed and I can't wait to root it out. In my opinion, I think mankind is destroying the planet, and my cancer is a symptom of environmental causes."

"Perhaps both genetics and the environment—pesticides, asbestos, arsenic, radon, etc. etc.—play a role. We'll see. Unfortunately, one in eight, or twelve percent, of all women—over their lifetime—develop breast cancer in the United States, and I think the situation is getting worse." He uncrossed his bad leg and rolled closer to the desk. "One of the genes we're going to test today is called the BRCA gene, and if that carries a gene mutation, then the risk of breast cancer in that individual is eighty-seven percent by the age of seventy."

Karissa leaned in and gasped. "That's crazy."

"And secondarily, if that gene is broken or mutated, then the risk of the second breast getting cancer is sixty-four percent by age seventy."

"Oh my God. I am so glad my oncologist referred me to you, Dr. Hookie. I will definitely ask the surgeon to do a bilateral mastectomy if I fall into this category."

"Smart woman. So, let's get started. First, I'm going to ask you details about your family history." He grabbed a piece of blank paper from the back of the printer and stuck a pen between his fingers. "We're going to dive into your family history. Ready?"

"Shoot."

After writing Karissa's name towards the bottom of the sheet, he circled it. "We're going to go backwards and develop a family tree, by asking you about your parents, your grandparents, aunts and uncles, etc. And do you have any children?"

"One girl. All grown up with her own children."

"This testing will also shed light for her. If you have the particular gene mutations we'll be testing for, it will increase your daughter's chances of breast cancer. And by the way, if you are positive, you may stand a chance of having higher risks for other cancers as well."

"Oh great. Thanks a lot."

Hook finished taking Karissa's history while she watched him draw a tree, linking family members together like limbs, and making circles of relatives. When she told him a relative had been diagnosed with cancer, he colored in a little circle for them. He turned the sheet around to face her. "Yes, you were at an increased breast cancer risk because of your maternal aunt's diagnosis, especially since she was so young. Genetic testing is warranted in your case."

Karissa looked up from his drawing with a pained expression. "She died in her forties. So do you need to draw my blood to send to the lab?"

"The samples we use are either from saliva or from blood. Your choice."

"I have an infusaport in my chest for drawing blood or for the IV infusions, but using my spit sounds a lot easier!"

Hook laughed. "You echo the sentiments of many." He pushed back from his chair, got up, and opened the steel storage cabinet behind him. After grabbing a box, he set it down, and rummaged through the contents.

"Here we go." Dr. Hookie pulled out a long vial from a plastic wrap and came around the desk. "You need to gather your saliva and spit into this vial. Fill it to this etched line," he pointed, "but bubbles and air don't count, so keep spitting until pure saliva comes up to that point and all the nonsense is above it."

"There's a first for everything. I bet few men ask ladies to spit for them, Dr. Hookie."

"Are you a Leonardo DiCaprio fan?"

Her face lit up. "Surely I am."

"He taught Rose how to spit on the deck of the Titanic."

"Now we're talking. I can get it up as good as them."

She finished and handed it over to Hook.

"Excellent."

"When will I get the results?"

"Sooner than most places. This is one of my areas of expertise, and I will run your sample myself in my lab."

CHAPTER 3

Hook finished with Karissa Larson, processed the paperwork involved with her testing, and wrote the full-time genetic counselor a note. He checked out the woman's pictures of her family scattered about the office, and thought about his own daughter. With only one kid, he wondered what it must be like to have several. His daughter was forty-one, but lived several states away. However, he often wondered if she was his only child. He had been foot loose and fancy-free those years serving in the military.

He closed the counselor's door behind him, and headed across the common area. Med students had poured out, presumably from a break between classes, and several threw Frisbees between them.

"Dr. Hookie, wait up."

Hook stopped as a man swiftly approached, his hair buzzed like an army guy wading in a trench. Wearing soft leather shoes, the man's gait was bouncy, and he halted with enthusiasm.

"I'm Kent Wadsworth," he said. "I have not had the pleasure of meeting you but, like everyone else around here, I know all about you."

"What can I do for you?" Hook asked, liking the man's snappy style.

"I'm the hospital's Associate Executive Director. I am overseeing this year's health fair and would like you and your area of expertise to partake in the festivities. It's tremendously educational for those attending. Most departments will partake in one way or another, and I'm making sure there are raffles and giveaways to get people really involved."

"Is this one of those fair type events where folks get free blood pressure screenings and diabetic skin pricks etc. etc.?"

"Yes. And just think. Most people don't know about genetic testing these days."

"Okay, of course. The whole campus will benefit, especially by a secondary financial gain due to all that exposure—if you are a stellar marketing man."

"Yes, sir. I hope so. There's nothing wrong with that. We do want our services to be on the forefront of patients' minds."

"I like your candidness. Are you only in your thirties to land that hospital title?"

"Yes, sir."

"No need to call me sir. Count me in. Put your idea for my department's participation in writing and send it to me. We'll probably be on the same wavelength."

"Thanks, Colonel, I mean Dr. Hookie."

Hook smiled, and shifted his weight off his bad leg. "I look forward to helping out and educating the public. Enjoy the day, son."

The young Mr. Wadsworth grinned back. As a Frisbee whizzed past him, a med student caught it on a fly, and Kent went on his way.

Down the last aisle, Cynthia and Alex barely peered up from their endeavors when Dr. Hookie returned. Engrossed, the couple worked together yet separate, and he felt blessed they collaborated in the same field as him.

He kept his silence and slipped to his back office. Little did Karissa Larson know it, but she would receive her DNA analysis much quicker than most people because he could personally run her analysis himself. He grabbed a root beer soda from his miniature refrigerator, and stepped back to the lab. His favorite aisle was the only one which ran parallel to the window, the sunlight streaming in and warming the counter top. A swig of soda went down smoothly as he contemplated starting this additional project.

First, he would use "NGS" technology—next generation sequencing—to test Karissa's DNA sequences. The cost in an outside lab would be an easy one-thousand dollars but, lucky for the patient, Hook could pass on a better price to her insurance company.

The next-generation sequencing costs had decreased since the completion of the Human Genome Project but, still, the machine to do it—the Illumina—had cost the facility a pretty penny. He had fought a good fight to be the benefactor of said funding.

He slipped the box out of his lab pocket which securely held the vial of saliva, and set it down. Looking beside it, a significant gasp heaved from his chest. The counter held a gap, the marble top showing a faint outline of dust where the desktop sequencer was supposed to be.

The pulse in his wrist bumped against the joint like it was revved up for a race. "No way," he said aloud, and hobbled as fast as possible over to Cynthia and Alex.

"Where the hell is the desktop Illumina?" As if commanding an air force unit, his stern voice carried authority. However, it was not with reprimand that he asked them, rather with disbelief and confusion.

Cynthia and Alex looked at him questioningly, and then at each other. "What are you talking about?" Alex asked.

"It's not back there."

"Maybe it's being repaired?" Cynthia questioned.

"Not that I'm aware, and I would know."

Alex squared his shoulders. "Was it stolen?"

Grimacing slightly, Hook shook his head in disbelief.

"If so, what did she cost us? Somewhere between twenty and fifty thousand dollars?"

Placing his hand on his forehead, Hook hid his expression. "Close enough," he said.

The brisk breeze from Lake Michigan filtered around the high rise buildings in downtown Chicago, causing Linda Sisko to grab the collar of her sweater tightly against her chest. She was a city girl by nature, but sometimes she wished the nearby freshwater behaved less like a sea and more like a lake. The influence of the current, depth, and crazy waves on the city, and the sustained winds, made hustling through the streets an extra chore. After all, she already had her hands full with her job of selling medical equipment to hospitals and health care places of business.

Linda was a perfect size six and wore her colorful clothes snugly like a model. Her hair, swiped back and held in a barrette, was a natural reddish-blonde, and the couple of freckles high on her cheeks matched her hair color.

"Maybe you can buy a coffee or something while I meet with him," she said to the man next to her. She switched the briefcase she held to the other hand and her words tumbled out of her mouth quickly, like the speed of someone throwing dice in a craps game.

The man next to her, her sidekick, was Dirk Crouch. He inhaled the cigarette between his fingers, a constant source of disapproval from the young woman, and nodded. "I'll pick another spot and order a real sandwich plate, if you don't mind."

"That'll work." Linda frowned as a whiff of smoke hit her in the face. She didn't know which she hated more—his chain-smoking, or his constant swiping of his nose, which was likely due to a tobacco allergy.

They turned into a noisy, small restaurant split into three sections. A stout man waved towards her from a booth, and she walked over while Dirk headed to the counter.

"I couldn't miss you in the pink sweater you promised to be wearing," the man said, shaking her hand. "I'm Bobby Hyland, the purchasing manager of the Illinois Hospital and Healthcare services."

"And I am Linda Sisko with 'Necessary for Healthcare.' Technically, I'm a salesperson, but everyone these days is upgraded to fancier work titles, so they call me a 'Technical Expert for Sales.' I think of myself as a pitch woman for items that are functional, necessary, and lifesaving in the industry of mostly health testing."

"Sounds appropriate to me. I have purchased from Necessary for Healthcare over the years, but never dealt with someone as pretty as you."

They slipped into the booth, and Bobby cleared his throat. "Uh, I'm sorry. I hope that didn't come as sounding sexist. I didn't mean it that way."

"No insult taken. Anymore, people get their panties in a wad with simple compliments, but I appreciate the remark. Better yet, make a hefty order today of medical equipment and I will appreciate you even more."

He laughed and leaned forward. "I went ahead and ordered lunch. Hope you don't mind. I'm on a tight schedule."

"I won't keep you. Let's get through the equipment we discussed on the phone." She opened a catalog from her briefcase and, as the waitress put down his food, he selected and finalized the list of needed items for the hospital.

Linda ordered the lunch combo of soup and salad, and when the server left to fill her request, she began writing him a receipt. "I can deliver these items next week, unless you want these items shipped which adds on a delivery charge." She poised her pen, waiting whether she should also add shipping and handling.

"I suppose nothing is too big to handle."

"My delivery guy who works with me is sitting at the counter. He manages with a dolly."

Bobby dug into his plate of pasta and gave her a slight thumbs up.

"Mr. Hyland, besides working for 'Necessary for Healthcare,' I also sell medical products on the side, on my own. They are usually machines and equipment which have been minimally used and returned to companies, and sometimes believed to be too unsalvageable to reuse. However, my associate and myself are whizzes at refurbishing equipment. We sell such products and, if our customers are not satisfied with a medical product we sell them, we will take it back within two weeks and return your money."

She silenced while the waitress put down her drink, and then added, "I'll make you sweet financial deals that you can't ignore—on dependable healthcare machinery that you must have."

"Really? My budget keeps getting tighter, particularly because of the rising cost of high-tech equipment."

Linda knew to strike like a snake when poised. "In your big, multi-medical centers and outpatient facilities, you can always use EKGs. Interested?"

Bobby slipped another noodle down his throat. "Absolutely. We're opening up an outpatient surgery center soon."

"I can sell them at one-half the price, and I will guarantee them. I can deliver you a half dozen by the end of the month."

He moved his drink glass out of the way as the server placed down Linda's items.

"Before you chow that down, tell me the brands you sell. And just in case we're not talking apples and oranges, the EKGs you're selling do work on human hearts, don't they?" He waited a second to watch her look of surprise, and then laughed. "I gotcha with that one, didn't I?"

"Yes, you did. If they don't work on humans, then I'll be sure to make more money selling them to vets. After all, veterinarians can afford equipment more than you can. They have high-paying cash customers, not like your colleagues in the hospital who need to fight with insurance companies to pay their customers or patients' bills."

She sprinkled salt and pepper on her soup, and picked up a spoon. "As far as brands, name the top three, and I probably have them in stock."

Impressed with the fast-talking female saleswoman who had two employers—herself and a major medical equipment company,—Mr. Hyland finished his lunch and picked up their tab.

Hook paced like a bobcat waiting to pounce as Cynthia and Alex stayed out of his way. "Crap," he said. "This puts a halt on a few of my projects."

The three of them had searched the lab for the missing next generation machine, even peering in every carton stored under the tabletops. Cynthia's eyes widened, and she twirled the pink piece of hair straggling the side of her face. "I'm sorry, Dr. Hookie."

He halted in front of her. "It's not your fault, Cynthia." Sometimes he wondered how he was fortunate enough to hire two young people who gave a damn. In his opinion, they were a rarity.

"Anybody in here?" Freddie Simpson turned the corner. Holding his head high, he smiled, and jostled a clipboard holding a clump of papers.

"Thanks for immediately popping up here," Hook said. "This is not about some lost EKG machine. An important asset of the campus' laboratory is missing. The machine which sat right here," he pointed.

"What was it?"

"Except for a minimum percentage of people, you wouldn't understand. Don't mean to be demeaning to you, Freddie. Here, hand me that—I'll fill in the description, model, and even the actual machine number which is etched underneath."

"Dr. Hookie, I'm a capable guard around here, but it sounds like we need to also report this to a higher authority."

Hook glanced up, not wanting to tell the guard that was a no-brainer. "I thought you could make the call while you're here."

Freddie shoved his blue shirt deeper into his pants. "Sure thing. I'll call the police department right now."

"Actually, want my opinion?"

"You're going to give it to me, Dr. Hookie. Whether I want it or not."

"The Atlanta area police department have their hands fuller than the number of French-style green beans in a sixteen-ounce can. No, I know a private detective in our region. Pulling her into this caper would assure us that this theft, or whatever it is, is given some kind of priority. It wouldn't be a 'report' shoved below a pile on the top of a cop's desk."

Freddie squinted his eyes and sighed.

"Don't worry," Hook assured him. "This won't reflect on your job performance."

"We regard you highly," Cynthia said, adding her soft woman's touch to the conversation. "It's always comforting to find you in a lobby doing your job, knowing your presence thwarts certain people from getting out of line."

"Yes," Hook nodded. "What she said. With your permission, let's go into my office, I'll dig up her number, and we'll both give her a call." He twisted his mouth in disgust. "Then I must drain more of this year's financial budget to purchase another desktop sequencer. I can't live without it."

CHAPTER 4

In his office, Hook dug up the phone number he needed from an old-fashioned Rolodex while Freddie scanned the shelves admiring the physician's pictures.

"Who is the private detective you're going to call?" Freddie asked, stuck looking at a photo of Hook's Air Force days.

"This person's background is as tightly wound as my own. Not only is she the snoopy detective I think she is, but she's also an M.D."

"No way. She's not practicing medicine?"

"Used to. Her transition to being a cop-like worker is a long story."

Hook put up his finger to halt their conversation and placed the call. After multiple rings, a woman answered. "Dr. Monaco," he said, "it's Dr. Hookie."

"How's life treating you, Hook?"

"Same old shit, just a different day."

"Glad to hear it. To what do I owe the pleasure?"

"Your services would be appreciated."

"I'm not seeing patients anymore, Hook."

"I couldn't care less about using you in that sense. How about helping me solve a caper?"

"Depends. What are we talking about?"

"An expensive piece of equipment disappeared straight out of my lab."

"Did you contact the police?"

"I want it solved yesterday, not in the next decade."

"You're not being fair to the police department."

"Who said I'm fair? Look, you're the perfect 'man' for the job. We can talk shop when it comes to the high tech medical equipment and jargon. If you come on board, I'll be speaking with someone who uses the same English as me, and I respect you because you know what you're talking about."

"But can you afford me?"

"Sydney, I'm as passionate as you are in what I do. You are *not* going to stiff me with a big bill."

She silenced on the other end. "Okay, Hook, you've got yourself a private investigator."

"Besides me, Monument Medical Center thanks you."

"You're welcome. I'll be over."

"You know where to find me."

Cynthia popped into the office and leaned against the windowsill near Freddie as Hook ended the call.

"You recruited her," Freddie said.

"Recruited who?" Cynthia asked.

"Help to solve our problem," Hook said, lowering his tall frame into his chair. He twiddled his thumbs and twisted his mouth. "What do you both want now?"

"Nothing," Freddie said. "Call on me for assistance and keep me posted about that investigator."

"Done." Freddie left and Hook stared at Cynthia. "Yes?"

"I can get your NGS analysis done this afternoon through my contact at Emory. He'll let me use their machine since ours is missing."

"You have the right contacts, Cynthia."

"They don't come close to the friendships you have maintained all these years. It's just that I thought to call him."

"But first I must isolate the DNA from the patient's saliva sample before you take it over there. Mind working late today?"

"No, you'll make it up to me some other day."

He ambled past her, nodded in agreement, and put other thoughts on his mind aside. That was easy because he loved all things DNA related. In the first biology class he ever attended, he was fascinated to learn that all living things carry DNA in their cells, and that the long molecule contained chains of nucleotides. The order of the nucleotides, he learned, was what made organisms similar to those in their own species, and yet different as individuals, and that the long molecule held sections called genes.

But, for scientists like him, he needed to get the DNA out of the cell to study it. What he wanted was 'pure' DNA. He needed to free it from its cell, and then separate it from the cellular fluid and proteins. Before giving a sample to Cynthia, he would carry out the basic three steps called lysis, precipitation, and purification.

Although Hook seethed over his machine being gone, he was glad the basic machinery was still in the lab. He set the spectroscopy unit on, and put the centrifuge unit on to work like a workhorse. Methodically paying attention and being redundant, he eliminated all the 'junk' not related to the DNA, and isolated the end product needed for the Illumina and the Microarray.

Hook took a big sigh, allowed himself a root beer break, and then wrote down Karissa Larson's name. He paid Cynthia a visit down her usual aisle. "Here you go—the patient's name and the sample to be tested over at Emory."

"Thanks. I'll be careful with this."

"Is he good-looking?"

"Who?"

"The guy over at Emory."

"Dr. Hookie, Alex and I…"

"Ah, ha. So you're not 'playing the field.' My lab assistants are serious about each other."

"Very clever of you," she said, shaking her head, "to elicit that information from me. Actually, Dr. Hookie, you are dating yourself. Most us young folks don't use that expression anymore when it comes to romantically or sexually being involved with several partners."

"Great. I've been told I'm not fair and I'm an old fogey all in one day, and the day isn't over. But I'll remember to discard 'playing the field' from my vocabulary."

"Yes, sir," she taunted him, wearing a smile. "And if you are also using the term 'old fogey,' then you are an old fogey."

"Hurry up. Get out of here before I fire you."

Another hour ticked by as Hook concentrated on the piles of work on his desk which had accumulated only because he hated doing that exact thing … taking care of paperwork. Opening and answering mail, and making phone calls, he realized he was getting a lot done. Someone stealing his machine, and Cynthia doing his patient's analysis somewhere else, had worked out to his benefit for the time being. Plus, he called the insurance company and informed them of his missing machine.

Someone artfully quiet came into his office and slipped into a chair before his desk.

"How are you doing, Hook?"

He snapped his head. "Sydney Monaco. Didn't expect you here today."

"I thought it best to see the 'crime' scene before anyone messes with it."

Hook rose, came around, and shook her hand. Like him, she had a slender build, and her aqua blue eyes sparkled with admiration for the retired Air Force Colonel and accomplished physician scientist.

He studied her face, like a mentor taking a student under his wings. "Anything new regarding the disappearance of your parents?

Sydney shook her head with disappointment. She and her twin brother had searched for the missing couple to no avail and the timely search, as well as the newfound interesting field she discovered, propelled her to make the career change from a practicing physician to becoming a private detective. Her medical knowledge and background gave her an edge over other PIs when it came to any crime related to healthcare.

"I'm sorry to hear that. Someday, a tip will come in about your parents' cold case, and the investigation will explode on the right track."

Sydney squinted her eyes. "Sometimes, I think the same thing. I hope so, but I'm not holding my breath. Right now, let's focus on your problem. Mine takes up enough energy lingering in the back of my mind like a buried bear in a winter den."

"You said the missing equipment is quite expensive." She glanced at his open paperwork. "You are filing an insurance claim, aren't you?"

"Yes, but I'm not telling the police department yet, unless you advise me to."

"I'll help you as much as I can, but trust me, you should tell them before they find out on their own." She frowned at his desk. "When you come up for air." She rose and added, "Show me where this machine was, and I'll need a picture."

Hook went to a file cabinet and handed her a pamphlet about the device. As they walked outside, he directed her to the empty space on the counter, and she glanced at the picture on the front cover of the brochure.

"It was plugged in back here?" She pointed to an outlet.

Hook nodded. She scanned above the counter, and then strolled around the entire periphery of the lab. Seeing Alex, she stopped.

"This is Alex," Hook said.

"Nice to meet you," she said. "I'll be back to talk to you."

She waved Hook to the entryway and glanced up at the ceiling. "Am I correct in my assumption that there are no cameras mounted in here?"

"Correct. Who would have thought?"

"That's the way it goes, Hook. When you least expect it, some devious human being finds a loophole, allowing their sinister schemes to materialize."

"But you can't prevent everything, Sydney."

"I agree." She poked her head into the hallway. "And no cameras in this hallway?"

"No."

"What is the routine to locking up this lab and your office overnight when you all leave?"

"My office is usually unlocked and this lab door is not always secured. We do have a security guard during the day and a fellow who works at night as well. They are dependable and are retired from the police department."

"But they can't be everywhere at the same time."

"So true."

"You look tired, Hook. When was the last time you left a few minutes *early*, went home, and put your feet up?"

"Can't say."

She tilted her head. "I'll talk to Alex and scout around downstairs. I'll take note of the first floors sweeping around the campus as well."

"I'm sure Susan will appreciate me getting home earlier than usual," he said, taking the hint.

"Say hello to her. Maybe we can all grab dinner one of these days."

"Will do," he said, and turned.

"Hook, what's the guard's name?"

"Freddie Simpson is the day guy. Come to think of it, he mentioned that an EKG machine recently vanished from a doctor's office on campus. That is a piece of equipment that could be easily misplaced, but under the circumstances, it makes me wonder."

"Exactly. I used to enjoy reading those P-QRS complexes. The memories sometime make me yearn…"

"Any chance you would consider practicing again?"

"No. I like what I'm doing too much compared to before."

Hook placed his hand on her upper arm. "Good night, then."

"You too, Hook."

Hook pulled his black Jeep into the garage and opened the house door. Bentley jumped off the nearby table, purred, and slunk across his forward path.

"I swear you think you're a dog," he said, crouching down and acknowledging him with a rub. "Let's go find Susan."

He pulled the band off his ponytail, as if relieving the pressure of the day, and saw his wife in her favorite chair.

"How was your day, honey?" She rose, and he gave her a kiss on the cheek.

"Fine as can be. I put that little slip collar leash on Bentley, and we took a walk around here. Plus, I did get to the cleaners to pick up your shirts."

"Your feet feeling okay today?"

"Yes, thanks for asking."

He narrowed his eyes at her, knowing when she fabricated her answers—which she only did when she wanted to protect him from worrying about her. Hook hated to watch her decline in recent years. After all, she used to be a competitive runner in her twenties, and now Type 2 diabetes had smacked shut her physical zest, and she had already suffered with a heart attack and two stents. That part of her history he blamed on a family history of early MIs. His own area of expertise—genetics—had an impact on his own wife.

But her feet were also cursed with a diabetic neuropathy, and her legs showed signs of varicose veins. Although he was four years older than her, his health shined in comparison. Plus, he did not carry the emotional baggage that she did. When he married her, he had no knowledge that she had issues which she needed to bury from her childhood. And whatever those aftereffects were, she kept her lips tightly sealed. Over and above all her issues, she was a pretty woman with a clear complexion, amber eyes, and sharp features.

Susan turned around and picked up her diet soda while Hook went to the refrigerator, pulled out a root beer, and snapped open the tab.

"How was work today?" she asked.

"Besides being called 'old,' 'unfair,' and verbally out-of-date, I'm dealing with a strange, new problem. It appears that one of my machines may have been stolen. I even called Sydney Monaco about it."

"Those names someone called you aren't true. And what's the world coming to if a scientific machine was stolen? How despicable."

"I agree."

"How's Sydney?"

"Fine. She said hello."

Hook took a swig of soda. Bentley circled his feet and kept glancing up at him. "All right, fella. I still didn't properly acknowledge you." He picked up the cat and cuddled him along his forearm.

"Susan, how about if I heat up the Thai leftovers from last night? It will have more flavor the second night."

"I'll warm our dinner up. Bentley needs you right now."

Hook made himself comfortable on a stool, nursed his soda, and held the cat while Susan scooped the leftovers into a pot. During dinnertime, he made occasional small talk to fill in his wife's ensuing quiet mood. When they bused the dishes to the sink, she finally commented, "You're a wonderful cook, Hook."

"So you say, honey, so you say." He rinsed and washed the plates while she dried and put them away.

CHAPTER 5

Hook stopped in the Campus Coffee and Bakery Shop and eyed the fresh muffins and bagels as the line moved forward. "How about three caramel lattes and three blueberry muffins?"

"Splurging today, Dr. Hookie?" the barista asked.

"I suppose so. Discourage Cynthia and Alex from buying anything this morning if they come by."

"You're the boss, but they've already come and gone."

At the cash register, he was handed a bag with the muffins and a cardboard cup holder with the specialty coffees. He turned right, passed the doctor's office building, and went to the elevators.

In the lab, Hook heard the running of machines. Cynthia and Alex faced each other across an aisle, talking and sipping from small take-out cups.

"Brought us a morning treat," he said, "but looks like I'm too late." He placed the items on the counter and popped the top off a latte.

"Thanks, Dr. Hookie," Cynthia said. She opened the bag and, with no hesitation, put a muffin on a napkin. "I have the Illumina results from yesterday."

"Thank you for going off site and doing that. I'll start working on the DNA deletions with the Microarray."

"Thank goodness that machine is still with us," Alex said. "Is your private investigator going to help out?"

"She's a busy lady handling other matters but, yes, she's going to help out."

Hook stayed and finished his coffee with them. They were solid, hardworking and smart lab technicians, and he was happy for them being together. They had a lot in common with each other, whereas other couples had such dissimilar interests, he wondered what they talked about.

He supposed his marriage qualified for the latter, with little in common, but he and Susan were old-timers, the way relationships used to work. Men worked, women stayed home, and that set up a barrier in and of itself. Living together in a marriage this long was based on a mutual, respectful, settling in of two individuals and getting along—an acceptance and complacency of each others deficiencies. Especially when the physical, sexual desire had long past. He loved his wife dearly and watched over her more than she knew, always wanting to somehow assure himself of her happiness.

"This muffin is delicious," Cynthia said. "Too bad. Now I'll have a difficult time at their counter—whether to buy one or not."

"The answer is clear," Alex said. "I'll splurge for you."

"No way. I'll decide on a day-to-day basis." Without a mirror, she readjusted the pink-streaked hair piece on the side of her head, and slipped the clip in.

"Off to work." Hook dumped the cup in the trash can, spent only a few minutes in his office, and went to the microarray machine. To run the analysis, he needed two things—Karissa's DNA sample and a 'control' or normal sample containing no mutation of the gene he was interested in.

First, he separated the two complementary strands of the DNA samples into single-stranded molecules, and then cut the long pieces into smaller fragments, easier to manage. He labeled the sections with a dye—Karissa's with green, and the control with red. In essence, after being inserted into the 'chip,' it was allowed to bind to the synthetic DNA.

The 'chip' consisted of a small glass plate encased in plastic, somewhat like a computer microchip. Each chip contained thousands of single-stranded DNA sequences—each one representing either a normal gene or the variant, mutated sequences known to exist in the human population.

If Karissa carries no DNA mutation, both colored samples would bind to the sequences on the chip which represents the sequence that is normal, without the mutation.

However, if Karissa did possess a mutation, her DNA would not bind correctly to the DNA sequences on the chip representing "normal" sequences, but instead would bind to the mutated DNA. He always thought of it as a lock and key. Mutated DNA would bind to mutated DNA but not normal DNA.

His morning sped by as he performed his analysis and ambled along the window aisle, making sure his leg didn't stiffen up.

Poring over Cynthia's results from the day before, and his own analyses, he made his determination.

Leaning against the windowsill, Dr. Hookie placed a call to Karissa. "Ms. Larson, this is Dr. Hookie at Monument Medical Center. I have the results of your genetic analysis. Would you prefer them over the phone, or would you like to come in and I can explain your situation in more detail?"

"This is all new to me. With my prior nursing experience, I would appreciate talking to you. Plus, I can stop in the OR and say hello to former colleagues."

"Like before, you can schedule an appointment at the cancer center. However, I'll be in my lab all day, and I won't mind if you pop in."

"You are so thoughtful. Yes, I'll stop by today."

Hook swung by Cynthia's aisle and leaned against the counter. "Want to take a pay cut, so I can scrounge up the money for a new NGS machine to replace the stolen one?"

She rolled her eyes and swung to face him.

"Not a fat chance."

"I don't blame you at all."

Hearing the thumping of approaching footsteps, Cynthia and Hook glanced over to find Freddie Simpson.

"Have you heard?"

"Heard what?" Hook asked.

"Sure makes us campus security guards look bad."

"Spit it out, Freddie."

"Several hospital EKG machines were stolen out of the storage room since yesterday and a radiologist's laptop computer vanished."

Hook stared at the floor, and pursed his lips. He hated and despised any unlawful behavior. "There's a hell of a shyster lurking around here. Crime has really ramped up, Freddie."

"The laptop makes more sense than your machine or the EKG machines," Freddie said. "You can stick one of them under your arm, walk away, and no one would suspect a thing. It was the radiologist's personal computer, so he's not too happy. He left it on his desk where he reads films."

"Did you talk to my PI yesterday?"

"Yes, she hunted me down. She asked some smart questions."

Alex's long legs brought him down the aisle and Freddie left. "Make sure you don't leave any personal possessions lying around," Hook warned him. "If and when Karissa Larson shows up, direct her back to my office."

Hook heard someone clear their throat as he sat in his office after lunch. Looking over, he saw Karissa Larson standing at the door. She pulled the newsboy's cap she wore off her head, not self-conscious about her hair loss.

"Come on in and take a seat." Before he could stand, she nestled into a chair. "Did you visit your old friends in the hospital?"

"Yes," she said and smiled. "They made my day. I was smothered in best wishes for my upcoming mastectomy."

"People sometimes underestimate the value of friendships from their work environment or, in your case, your previous place of employment."

"So true. What did you find out, Dr. Hookie?"

"Your results may impact your final decision. You told me you scheduled a unilateral mastectomy, and that changing the surgery to a double mastectomy was always a possibility."

He reached to the outer corner of his desk and pulled forward a file. "Glad you came in. Makes my day to explain this to someone who's interested and wants more than the bottom line."

Hook leaned forward and tapped on a diagram. "So, up to twenty percent of all breast cancer is due to a hereditary cause. I mentioned the gene before, but up to fifty percent of that genetic cause is due to a gene or genes we call BRCA1 and BRCA2—pronounced Bracca. You do not have a broken, mutated BRCA gene."

Karissa's eyebrows lifted and she grinned.

"This has a bearing on other associated cancers because if this gene was mutated, you also would have had a higher risk of ovarian cancer, as well as a higher association with pancreatic cancer, a melanoma, and prostate cancer if you were a male."

"I'm off the hook!"

"More than that. It means you don't have the defect to pass on to a child." He leaned back against the wall, the front legs of his chair dangling in the air. "This does not mean a daughter or son is off the hook, however, because their father could carry a defect."

"I have a daughter, Dr. Hookie, so this news is reassuring."

"BRCA is not the only gene I tested you for. There are others, many others, six of which are quite important as well, such as the CHEK2 gene. If that one is broken, add in a danger of acquiring a colorectal cancer." He dropped his chair back down. "I won't bore you with anymore. The bottom line is that you were negative on all counts and your siblings don't warrant testing either."

"So does this mean I had bad luck getting breast cancer?"

"When we eliminate these hereditary and familial factors, what's left are 'sporadic' cases. Maybe the environment, chemicals, toxins, and one's lifestyle, are to blame. But I can assure you this, scientists and lab techies are making strides every day in pinpointing more abnormal genes."

"Thank God for people like you. To a layperson, it seems like boring work, but you people have utmost patience and knowledge to pursue your work under a microscope and these technical machines."

"Thank you."

Her face lit up with the final realization that she could be assured of her previous decision. "Since I have no hereditary factors involved with my cancer, it would make sense to not have a double mastectomy."

"I agree. If you had a mutation, then you also had a high risk of acquiring a cancer in the second breast."

"What would you do, Dr. Hookie?"

"If I were a woman in your shoes, I would keep the second breast. And I would have a full mastectomy on the first breast, not a lumpectomy."

Karissa's face softened, relieved that Hook shared his opinion, and satisfied that he felt the same way as her. She stood and lingered while he also rose and handed her the genetic results in an envelope.

"I can't thank you enough, and for personally expediting my testing."

"No problem. I'll show you to the door. I need to stretch anyway."

They walked side-by-side. "Cancer is a terrible thing," she said. "Before I was advised to do testing, I thought strongly that mine was caused because I did too much mixing up and spraying of weed killer last summer. It's the first time I made up spray bottle after spray bottle of the stuff because the weeds were as bad as Kudzu."

"That may be your answer. I'm sorry, but good luck with your surgery and come back and visit us any time."

She clutched the envelope, slipped her cap back on, and strolled down the hallway.

Rachel Foreman grasped her to-go cup in one hand, and her briefcase in the other as she entered the stately Chicago bank where she worked. With mid-length, blond curly hair, and blue-green eyes, she qualified as a pretty, single, thirty-one-year old.

Fortunately for her, she carried all the enthusiasm of a young person satisfied with their job, but it had taken a while for her to get there. Her past was riddled with trauma, so she had mistakenly thought she would derive satisfaction by training to become a police officer. After enrolling in the Chicago Police Academy, she realized that was not for her. She didn't want to subject herself to the violence that cops face on the job, particularly in a city like Chicago.

Her short heels click-clacked across the shiny floor as she made her way to her desk. It wasn't that she gave up on solving criminal activity. Even as a child, Rachel had loved reading old Nancy Drew books, and she often thought of herself as an amateur sleuth, like her mother Ellie. After quitting the Police Academy, the opportunity to eventually become a bona fide fraud investigator for the bank arose. Fraud was so interesting to her since the crimes were more subtle than outright robberies. She would train as a personal banker, and if she did well, they'd promised to promote her to the fraud department.

Escorting a woman beside him, the bank manager headed her way. "Good morning, Rachel. Everyone in their offices are tied up already. Would you mind taking care of our customer? This is Linda Sisko."

"I would be happy to. I can work and drink coffee at the same time."

"That's more than I can do," he said with a smile.

Rachel steadied her swivel chair and sat while Linda pulled her chair up close.

"I like your barrette," Rachel said. "Now, what can I do for you?" She slipped the lid off her coffee to let it cool.

"I have a pay check I'd like to deposit." She handed over a check and deposit slip.

Rachel managed bank teller transactions, but she figured the manager sent her over for more than one reason. She peered at the papers.

"Yes, I wish that pay check was better," Linda said. "I work for 'Necessary for Healthcare' selling their equipment, but they pay me a flat salary. I wish my pay was based on commissions because I'm an above-average pitch woman, and would make more money that way."

Rachel studied the fast talking woman, her freckles, and high cheekbones. "I suppose not working on commission makes you sell and hustle less." She shrugged. "Human nature, I suppose."

"So true. However, what you have is my pay to put into that account. What I want to do is open a separate account as well. Kind-of like for the things I do sell on commissions."

Rachel tilted her head, as if questioning her. "You are industrious if you have another employer."

"My commission work is because I'm self-employed."

Rachel opened her computer and began logging in Linda's first deposit. "If your side line isn't for this company," she asked, reading the name of Necessary for Healthcare, "whose equipment do you sell?"

"Oh, well… just refurbished machines. Sometimes hospitals are willing to part with old equipment. I mean, Necessary for Healthcare gives me old stuff not usable anymore."

Although Rachel seemed intent on the computer screen before her, she listened carefully and came to the conclusion that the woman before her talked in circles about what she did.

"That transaction is finished," Rachel said. "Do you have a deposit for the account you want to open?"

Linda handed over a check written out to her—more money than her paycheck.

"Should I open this account in your name only, like the other one?

"Yes, I'm single. Only my name, please. Do make it another checking account. I need to pay a guy that helps me out."

Being the sleuth that she'd grown up to be, she smelled a fishy customer. But there was nothing that raised her suspicions about any kind of bank fraud going on. Leave it alone, she told herself. She finished her client's paperwork, handed her the deposit tickets and new checkbook, and wished her a good day.

When the customer left, Rachel peeked again at Linda Sisko's name as well as the name of her employer. The coffee tasted bad when she contemplated the vagueness of the woman's other 'job.'

CHAPTER 6

Besides the sheer aroma of coffee being brewed, and the taste of a fine latte sliding down her throat, Belinda Sisko was keen on nibbling the chocolate chip biscottis at the Campus Coffee and Bakery Shop. In her opinion, Monument Medical Center had a mediocre cafeteria with watered-down coffee and lousy baked goods, so she frequently sat at a round table in the coffee shop between the hospital and doctor's office building.

Another thing Belinda approved of was that people came and went, almost always in a hurry, so that seemed to cloak a person sitting there in anonymity. Straight from being a teenager to her adult life, she never qualified as an extrovert, yet she wasn't shy either.

Belinda could talk up a storm when she wanted to but, overall, she shied away from group activities, or making small talk with others. That was one reason she liked social media platforms or cell phone texting. A person could engage with other people only when and if they wanted to.

She was a slim five-foot eight woman who could shop through a size six clothes rack, yet sometimes she needed more length in her clothes and had to be particular about sticking with brand names that catered to tall women. At forty-one, she thought she was getting old, and had no idea where her thirties went. Best to savor every day, she thought, as she envied the young women popping in for their to-go cups who were medical students, residents, or attending physicians. She assumed they had the perfect lives and commanded respect wherever they went.

But to Belinda, college was enough and, in addition, most of her business sense came from street smarts, not from books. These days, too many people were intent on being professional students. All they did was advance from degree to degree like they wanted to accumulate letters behind their names—nowadays, most folks didn't even know what all those letters stood for.

Belinda wore a few freckles on her upper cheekbones but, unlike her twin sister Linda, she carried a subtle birth mark off to the left side of her eye. She nibbled on the biscotti and wondered if Linda was up and about yet; her sister never had as high an energy level as her. However, even

Belinda was a bit under the weather these days.

Her sister lived in Chicago, and she missed having Linda closer. After all, neither of them was married, neither of them had children, and they were as thick as thieves.

The twins thievery started innocently enough. They had an older brother and, when they were born, their mother never expected two babies, and wasn't psychologically prepared. After all, the boy, Kenny, was the apple of the father's eye, and they exposed the youngster to basketballs, golf clubs, and hockey sticks. The girls were coddled and kept separate from the son's activities like they had the flu.

When the twins turned eight years old, their lunchtime consisted of eating a grilled cheese sandwich at home almost every day, and then they walked back to school. Their mother watched her weight like a Times Magazine top model, and because she didn't want to be tempted, she refused to keep sweets in the house.

"Here you go," Mrs. Sisko said every Monday through Friday. "Buy yourselves a candy bar on the way back to school." She handed them both a coin and waved them out the door.

The neighborhood mini-store was smack in their path back to the elementary school. Belinda and Linda stood together in front of the candy bar rack. "What are you getting?" Belinda asked.

"The usual." Linda plucked out a plain chocolate bar. "What about you?"

"Same as every day." She grabbed a chunkier candy bar, covered in chocolate, but with a soft, nutty center. But she stood staring forward at the entire rack.

"What's the matter?"

"I really want one of those chocolate covered coconut bars. We should get one and split it."

"How? We don't have enough money."

Belinda's eyes were like lightning, scanning the shopkeeper who knew them well, and the surrounding area. Like a lizard's tongue, her hand shot out, picked up the Mounds bar, cupped it in her hand, and into her pocket it went.

Linda gasped, and then giggled. They stepped to the register and handed the manager their money. He smiled, and they stepped outside.

"I can't believe you did that!" Linda exclaimed, and peeled back her candy wrapper. "I didn't think you wanted candy that much. I mean, you stole something. You just became a thief."

Belinda shuddered, but then she smiled. No one ever labeled her anything before, and being called a definitive name made her feel important.

"What are we going to do with the extra candy bar?" Linda asked.

"After school, I'm putting it under my pillow. Before going to bed tonight, we can split it."

That night, the two girls sat on the floor between their beds, the door closed, and munched on the coconut bar. "This is so good," Belinda said, "and Mom will never give us anymore additional money for candy. Next time, it'll be your turn."

"Yeah, she'll pay for another karate class for Kenny, but we're lucky if she gets us a Y membership."

"She won't. The YMCA is in the opposite direction of Kenny's activities."

The petty thievery continued. After the girls slipped through puberty and became young teenagers, it ramped up to stealing make-up and clothes. Not that their mother paid much attention to their closets, but they carefully didn't steal too many items to raise her suspicion.

However, the day came when they thought up their most successful heist to date.

It was a dead-of-winter weekend. The snow fell softly from the sky, like soft baby pillows, as the girls stared out from a ski lodge, mesmerized by a smooth, snowy slope. Like many other students on their campus, they were going to try out the most popular sport in the region.

"Let's go," Belinda said. They trudged through the base of the slope to the rental equipment shed, and were equipped with all the basics. Belinda signed for both sets of skis, poles, and boots.

"Where do we go for our first lesson?" she asked the young man who outfitted them.

"Right outside the door. At the moment, a decent skier is finishing a lesson. Like sex," he said with a straightforward glance, "enjoy your first time."

The girls took to skis like ducks to water. They snowplowed like beginners, but soon graduated to side-to-side motions on the beginner's slope.

"Come back for more lessons when you want to further pursue these slopes," their instructor said when they'd finished their class. He left them at the base of the slope and walked off to his next customer.

"I could use a hot chocolate," Linda said, "so let's get our sneakers back and return this equipment."

"Those cheap things? No, follow me." Belinda pushed along on the skis in the opposite direction as the shed.

"Where are you going?"

"Shut up and follow me."

Belinda scanned the front of the ski lodge and the parking lot as they slid past, and kept going. At her car, she took off the equipment and stood on the snow with her thick socks. After wiggling the skis across the seats from back to front, she waved quickly at Linda for hers.

Linda imitated her sister. "Sometimes I don't know how you come up with these ideas," she said as both of them jumped into the car. She needed to crunch near the door and couldn't fasten her seat belt due to the intrusive skis and poles. Belinda listened but didn't acknowledge her sister as she pressed on the gas pedal only wearing socks.

"I don't think we can use this rental equipment again at this slope," Linda warned her while placing her hands over the warm air blowing out from the car vent.

"No problem. We can camouflage them with stickers or something and, more than likely, use them at another ski slope."

The girls stopped at a coffee shop on the way back. "That was ridiculously easy to pull off," Belinda said. "Maybe we can do that again, and sell used ski equipment on campus."

"You mean stolen, used ski equipment," Linda retorted, "Perhaps we can, but first let's allow the dust to settle."

"You mean the snow." Belinda chuckled and paid for both their hot chocolates.

Belinda hung around the medical campus quite a lot, especially the

39

coffee shop. She was all ears as Kent Wadsworth, with his exuberant gait, came in and stopped short. He considered the menu while a campus worker dressed in a dark shirt and trousers followed him in.

"Mr. Wadsworth, when do you want me to hang those new pictures in the lobby?"

"There's no hurry. We are doing a face lift on two of the campus lobbies in time for the health fair, which has been an ongoing planning project for me. My goal is to make the event the best one yet."

"Along with my two other guys, we'll help out as much as possible."

"Just hold those paintings in storage until I tell you to spring them out. They are expensive."

"More expensive than that spectacular sculpture gracing the entrance?"

"No, we're not talking those kinds of big bucks." He softened his voice. "But still worth a few thousand."

The worker squinted his eyes. "Is that wise? Putting them out there?"

"Not a problem. The frames are big and bulky and someone sits at the reception desk all the time. This is a medical campus, not a hit-and-run grand scale museum for art theft."

"People probably don't get away with that kind of stuff anyway."

Kent Wadsworth shook his head. "Are you kidding? Art theft is lucrative. Few important pieces are ever recovered. Look what happened in Boston ten or twenty years ago—a theft of the magnitude of five-hundred million dollars."

"I never heard about that. All I remember in the news is that stupid painting which was stolen called *The Scream*. They ended up recovering that one. Anyway, Kent, I'll be around. Just give me a holler."

Kent nodded, placed his order, and left. Belinda left her things on the table and stepped over to a magazine rack. She brought back the hospital's monthly black and white thick newsletter. Looking at the front inside cover, she scanned the names of the main hospital executives, and found a "Kent." Kent Wadsworth was the Associate Executive Director of Monument Medical Center. She was beginning to know so many people on campus, yet few, if any, really knew who she was—most of the time.

Fifteen minutes later, with the second cup of coffee in her hand,

Belinda gave a small wave to a hawk-nosed man with a square chin who walked into the shop. Duane Harper slipped between two round tables, and pulled out a chair. Like her, he was forty-one years old, but to his detriment, he wore a tattoo to the side, and the bottom of his neck. At least she considered it to be a disadvantage; people on the wrong side of the law shouldn't carry a distinguishing mark or sign on their bodies.

"I wish you'd get rid of that anchor plastered on the base of your neck," she said softly.

"So you've said. I like my tattoo. I wear more than the one on display, you know."

"I bet. I don't care what body parts you wear them on, as long as it's not an insignia in plain sight—drawing attention to you."

"Let's drop it, Belinda."

"I have an idea." She rummaged through her purse, and pulled out a cosmetic. "Rub some of this skin makeup on it before coming here and roaming around the medical center."

Duane grasped the small bottle filled with a light brown skin toner. "For once, you're making sense about my tattoo, offering a solution rather than insinuating that I rip the thing off my skin."

"I'm glad. Maybe we can start this morning off again from the start. How about I buy you a coffee?"

He gave her a slight downward hand wave, bought his own, and sat back down.

"Duane, before you arrived, I overheard an interesting conversation that may be of benefit to us."

"I'm listening."

"The hospital is organizing some kind of health fair on the premises, and there are plans to add some new, expensive artwork in the lobby. Maybe the pictures can disappear before they are hung." She added a chuckle and a glance around the place.

"I saw a flier about that. I could use a free medical check."

"Yes, me too, and I will. But what do you think about the paintings or whatever they are?"

"I think you're crazy. We're in the medical equipment resale business." He emphasized 'resale' and laughed.

"Duane, you need to be more open-minded and progressive. We could always steal artwork and store them. We'll find out how to dispose of them properly. Plus, the campus police are now thinking about medical equipment vanishing, not decorations for the lobby!"

Duane dumped a sugar in his coffee and stirred. "What's the definition of 'properly?'"

"The more dollar signs the better."

"There are art auction sites, you know. They work via the internet. All you have to do is submit pictures, descriptions, etc."

"See? There you go! Once they are stolen, the associate executive director of the hospital isn't going to be looking for them on an art auction site." She tapped her finger on his name in the hospital paper. He'll probably consider the stolen works part of an operating loss. After all, they aren't worth mega bucks, just mini bucks."

"All right. If, and I mean if, it is convenient for us, and if it appears to be a safe job to pull off, then we'll do it. Are you going to tell your sister? Or consider off-loading them to her to sell?"

"No. I'll see what I can do myself with your online art auction idea. If that doesn't work, I'll let her take them off our hands."

They sat in silence, Duane finished his coffee but, instead of leaving, he nodded towards a man and woman who walked in close together and stepped in line.

CHAPTER 7

Duane Harper furrowed his brow. Half of what he pulled off with Belinda Sisko was because of their attentiveness and the information they acquired all over the medical campus. And there was no better place to eavesdrop than the coffee shop and the cafeteria.

By positioning themselves near tables or lines where important employees or people in charge frequented, they learned that people do not curb their conversations, nor the volume of their discussions between each other.

One day in the cafeteria, Duane overheard a CT scanner tech brag to someone on the phone, "Administration just gave us a brand-new scanner with all the bells and whistles, the best technology money could buy. I'm a techie who likes learning the latest equipment, and I hate boring jobs, so you won't lure me to your hospital."

When he and Belinda Sisko started in this business, tying their efforts across the miles to Belinda's sister, Linda, and her side-kick Dirk Crouch, their learning curve needed to move exponentially. They could only make money if they were careful and learned how the system worked.

With the tech bragging in the cafeteria, Duane realized ancillary equipment must have been purchased along with the CT scanner. Most of the money spent in medicine, they had learned, did not go towards "big ticket" items, but the largest expense for the medical campuses went towards labor. Capital medical equipment was a small part of their budget, but then disposables were a significant cost, often exceeding the major devices.

Based on overhearing that conversation, Belinda scoured the imaging area, her eyes sharp, focusing with attention to every device and detail that she could.

Seemingly insignificant to the unbeknownst patient, Monument Medical Center had the latest and greatest ramps and scissor-lifts next to the CT machine's moving table. It was the necessary, and most up-to-date equipment to raise wheelchair users close to the transfer surfaces.

A few phone calls later, Belinda and Duane had the heist figured out. Slightly camouflaged, and looking like a generic hospital worker, Duane went from a man's bathroom in the hall of the radiology department, to the scanner room during the tech's lunchtime. With two hands, all he did was roll the new ramp out, down the service elevator, and to his waiting van in the back loading area of the hospital.

On his next drive to Chicago, Linda and Dirk took possession of the item. It found a new home in the city's health care system through Linda's reselling of stolen medical equipment, easy because of her real job and contacts through "Necessary for Healthcare."

A few more folks entered the coffee shop, and Duane leaned closer to Belinda. "Art work is one thing, but let's not lose sight of what we really do." He tipped his head toward the line, and slipped to the next table, close to the two people in the middle.

A hospital volunteer wearing a bright orange jacket smiled at him. "Want to step in front of me? I'm not in a hurry," she said.

He shook his head. Interested in the two lab technicians in front of her, he knew where the woman with the pink streaked hair worked and the man with her. Cynthia, Alex, and Dr. Hookie's laboratory genetic testing machine was still in his van, ready for his next run to Chicago.

Duane wanted a fuller, more lucrative cargo load, he thought, before getting on the road towards the western metropolis. Atlanta's traffic was bad enough but, he hated with a passion, the road closures, delays, and crazy drivers in Illinois.

"What are you getting today?" Alex asked Cynthia. He squarely faced her and ran his index finger over a sliver of her long streaked hair.

"Are you buying?"

"For you, always."

"I'll have a mocha whatever."

"Let's buy grande coffees to start the day off with a bang. It'll be an upbeat morning because Dr. Hookie's replacement machine should be delivered."

"That will make it easy on me too. I won't have to run over to Emory to use their NGS machine."

"Really?"

"What do you mean 'really?'"

Alex smiled, keeping his focus on her. "I sweated it out the other day— you being over there, near some man who may be of 'interest' to you."

"Oh, him. Don't worry," she said, her expression unchanged. "We had a quickie in the lab's storage room, so now I'm over him."

"Perfect," he said, playing along. "Now you know you're with the best. There are no more comparisons to be made." He clutched her hand and squeezed, and they took a step up in line.

Duane pushed his chair back, and Alex glanced back at him, a man sitting alone at a table without any coffee. Alex was sure that man heard them. Weirdo, he thought, the guy had nothing else better to do, and noticed the tattoo on his neck.

"What can I get you?" the barista asked.

"Two mocha lattes," he said, and focused on the pastry items in the glass case.

Duane stood, and put his back to the coffee line. "Belinda, I think we have a pre-takeoff this morning."

Belinda widened her eyes. "Pre-takeoff" was their buzz word when a "job" was imminent. However, as far as she knew, they had no imminent heist that day.

"You better leave," she whispered. "We've been near each other too long already. Text me."

He spun on his heels and outside the shop and building. His fingers darted across his iPhone keyboard. *"Those lab geeks in line said Dr. Hookie is getting a 'replacement' machine this morning?!"*

"Wow. Snatch it before it even gets upstairs?! Where's your van?"

"Soon to-be near the loading dock."

"Okay. Pre-takeoff confirmed. I will cover for you. What a way to spend a morning."

Duane only responded with a thumbs-up emoji. Belinda bounced back in line, and bought a new cup of coffee to keep her company in the back area of the campus when the time came.

First, Duane circled his car from the front of the campus to the back, driving slowly to monitor every section for any outside law enforcement vehicles. He parked near a loading zone, but far away enough from the back entrance of the emergency room. While still in his van, he grabbed his shirt collar and flipped it up to obscure his tattoo, and selected one of three baseball caps he had sitting on the passenger seat. After adjusting it on his head, he stepped outside into the overcast day.

Duane, well acquainted with the loading dock areas of the campus, scanned and walked the sidewalks and parking lots like a true thief stalking out a preliminary bank heist. There was normal activity—a small truck with a man unloading food for the cafeteria, a larger truck with two men removing hospital supplies, and two garbage trucks picking up rubbish. One was for the necessary disposal of needles and sharps—waste collected in red square containers that hung on walls in patient's rooms, ICUs, and especially the OR.

Over time, he was becoming more observant and, more and more, he was gaining more satisfaction from his job. Not just because of the money, but because of the ability to do something foxy and cunning, and get away with it. The euphoria he experienced was like a drug.

Most importantly for his outside campus heists, however, was the one and only security camera which was hung above the entrance to the emergency room. Mounted on one frame, two cameras jutted out, one facing to the right and one to the left. He assumed the main purpose was to monitor that back entrance to the hospital because of the trauma and medically unstable patients coming in by ambulances. However, quite a bit of the loading and unloading of trucks was in the cameras' range of sight.

Duane appeared innocent as he walked around, stopped on a curb, and pulled out a pack of cigarettes. Which is what he hated—pretending to smoke. He was never a smoker and deplored the habit, but once in a while, it was one of his props. Lighting up, and taking a puff, he wasted time back and forth to his van, waiting for the right delivery truck, as well as the right time to text Belinda to alert her, so she could show up and watch his back.

Within an hour, he spotted the small truck which captured his interest, and he texted her. She slipped through the ER back hallway, headed for the exit door.

Hook peeled away from setting up two centrifuges at the same time, and stepped away from the low sound of the spinning machines. Besides all his other duties, he went to his computer and continued with a research paper he was working on. In the entire campus area, as well as Atlanta, he was the most published medical doctor, setting statistics from DNA studies as gold-standards. The work created stepping stones for mankind's future manipulation of genes. Someday, he figured, genetic diseases would be wiped out. Often, he thought of sickle cell disease. During his lifetime, he harbored a secret wish to eradicate that predicament for any future patients.

Lost in his compilation of statistics on a grid, an hour passed in a second. His right leg was stiff, he pinched himself to stand and move about, and to grab a root beer from the small refrigerator in the corner.

He almost dropped it as loud electronic beeps sounded over the campus loudspeakers. The public address system alerts stopped after two of them, but they were followed by a short, distinctive announcement.

"Baby at door," it declared, loud and flat.

Cynthia popped her head in, with Alex beside her. "What is that?" she asked.

Hook shot her a worried glance. "It means someone just made off with an infant from the newborn nursery. A baby was snatched."

"Oh my God."

"Never heard that before," Alex said.

"It's rare, but it happens. Last one was before you two started working here. The hospital prepares for such a high alert, all significant employees understand what it means, and they are trained to respond. Security guards are now casing the exits and local law enforcement is simultaneously being called."

Cynthia wrung her hands. "Is there anything we can do?"

"No. Say a prayer, cross your fingers, or do whatever is your modus operandi for a higher power to help. The future life of an individual is at stake."

Belinda's foot stepped on the rubber floor pad of the ER and the automatic doors slid open. Two loud signals sounded over the public address system, so she stopped. It would be best to know if there's an emergency going on like a fire, she thought, because anything could deter her and Duane's hopeful, and imminent robbery.

"Baby at door," some female voice said. She turned, wondering what that meant. What baby? At what door?

She hurried outside and scoured the area with narrowed eyes. Luckily, she made eye contact with Duane, who leaned against a pillar by one of the loading docks. He nodded towards two older men popping out of a small truck, one scanning a clipboard of papers while the other one opened the vehicle's back door.

The door behind her opened again, and a man rushed out with black trousers, and a blue shirt with a silver security badge. He bumped into her, but she couldn't decipher if he did it on purpose. Afraid he may knock into her again, she put her hand on the top of her head and held it down.

Freddie Simpson took one step back and surveyed her up and down. Her hand grasped a cell phone, and a miniature purse with a shoulder strap hung by her side. There was no stolen baby in her arms.

"Did anyone just come out these doors holding an infant?" he asked.

"No. Not at all. It's clear back here," she added, wanting no extra surveillance of the loading dock areas.

The sound of sirens approached and blared as two police vehicles jerked into the parking lot from the adjacent back street. One veered to the right, and one to the left. When they stopped, a passenger officer jumped out of each one. With two police vehicles now sliding up towards the entrances, two officers were now on foot watching for a kidnapper with a bundle in their arms.

At first, Duane bit his lip, hating the sudden police presence. Certainly, it had nothing to do with him, he thought. He had yet to steal the NGS machine. Some other emergency was going on, and if he knew anything about stealing, it was that a diversion is a great enabler for a successful heist. Thieves usually had to invent their own diversion, but his was landing at his feet without him having to concoct it!

The two men from the truck finished moving their designated delivery to the lip of the door and stopped. Their eyes followed the commotion. "Come on," one of them said, "let's ask him what's going on." He pointed to one of the cops one aisle over and hustled over.

Duane ditched his first plan to sign for the genetic testing machine at the loading dock platform. He stepped to their vehicle, picked up the square machine in his arms, and backed off to the side of the truck. A few more steps and he was at his van. Just like Belinda's shoplifting instinct, he sensed what he should do. Pushing back the front passenger seat, he placed the machine carton on the floor, got into the vehicle and eased out of his space. As he approached the second officer on foot, he stuck a piece of gum in his mouth. He flipped off his baseball cap, stuck it under his seat, and replaced it with a vibrant orange one from the storage area at the bottom of the driver's door. A bright, distinctive, or crazy-looking cap, he had learned, makes another person focus less on the hat wearer's facial features.

The officer jerked his palm up, asking Duane to stop.

Duane finished rolling down his window. "What's the problem, officer?"

"Get out, open the passenger door as well as the back. A baby has been stolen from the hospital."

Duane did as he was asked. The officer saw a heavily sealed box up front, gave it a little tilt to make sure it didn't feel or cry like a baby. The box was heavy, so he quickly scoured the back of the vehicle—empty except for a bit of dust.

Time was of the essence for the cop. He nodded at Duane and waved him on.

Outside the ER door, Belinda sighed with relief as Duane drove away. And now she had a ring-side seat for when the two men stepped back to their vehicle to finish their delivery.

CHAPTER 8

In the parking lot, the two men from the truck carrying Hook's NGS machine spoke with one of the police officers. Finding out that someone had stolen a baby, they made a promise to him to keep their eyes peeled for someone carrying an infant. The policeman jumped back into the cop car with his colleague and drove around to the other side of the hospital.

One of the delivery men paused and lit a cigarette. "Can you imagine that? I don't want kids because I don't make enough to support myself let alone someone else. Why would someone steal someone else's child? Babies are an expensive and time-consuming item to snatch."

His buddy waited for the puff of cigarette smoke to hit the air. "Come on, we left the truck door open. I have one kid and, yeah, they cost a lot, but they're worth it. You'll be sorry someday when you're old and wobbly, and have nobody to call on the phone to tell them you love them."

"What you're describing doesn't sound all that worthwhile to me."

His colleague rolled his eyes, stepped away, and his buddy followed. At the truck, both back doors stood ajar. Looking at the lip of the vehicle, the two men jerked their heads toward each other.

"What the hell?" the man with the cigarette cried.

"No way. Maybe someone from the loading dock grabbed the box to keep it safe. Hurry, let's go."

At the platform, a man shook his head vehemently. "We haven't taken one thing off of somebody's truck without their permission."

Meanwhile, Freddie Simpson had walked away from Belinda Sisko and continued on his independent scouring of the area for a kidnapped infant. Especially since the police force was present roaming around the campus in two or more vehicles, it was important for him to proceed on foot. He stepped onto the loading dock next door, and the two delivery men stopped him.

"We need your help," the nonsmoker said. "It appears that the delivery item we're dropping off to a doctor just disappeared from the back of our truck."

Freddie scratched his chin. "Really? But this is bad timing. At present, something more important is taking up our energies." His head bobbed, assuming they'd heard the police car sirens.

"Okay," the smoker said. "We'll leave a report with the office inside."

The security guard stepped away, justified with the importance of the present situation. It brought him back to his real career days before his police force retirement.

Belinda kept her head down. Toeing in her right foot, she stepped toward her car with a great sense of accomplishment. She couldn't wait to text her sister that she and Dirk would be receiving another shiny new NGS machine in their next shipment.

Being a professional, and having been in charge of men in the Air Force, Hook Hookie held onto his composure. In no way was he going to lash out at the people responsible for the delivery and pick up of his Next Generation Sequencing DNA machine with a fiery assault of words. How would that help with what had transpired? The damage was done.

Of course, he was silently furious after the call from the loading dock that the machine was nowhere to be found, gone from the delivery truck in their own parking lot. This meant he needed to start from scratch all over again to procure his equipment.

However, at least, he thought, the actual acceptance of the machine by the facility had not occurred. It was stolen before being officially owned by the campus, so he had no need to place an insurance claim.

Hook barely sat all morning, pacing around like an unsettled cat looking for shelter, keeping his right leg moving. He swung the door open to the small refrigerator and pulled out an overdue root beer soda and poured it into his plastic cup. Staring at the blue letters of the sign on his shelf—Monument Medical Center—he figured the search for a baby had gotten less fanatical, and he picked up his cell phone and dialed the two people he needed. One more than the other.

"Freddie," he said, "meet me in the cafeteria at five o'clock. My NGS machine was stolen again."

A pause ensued and Hook thought he was disconnected. "Uh…, I heard about a machine being stolen, but I didn't know it was yours. You're having bad luck, sir. I'm sorry."

"Not your fault, Freddie. A thief or multiple thieves are quite intelligent about the value of medical equipment, and must have a 'lay' of the land. Or so it seems. A more important matter was on everyone's agenda today. Any luck finding the snatched infant?"

"No, not at all."

"How awful." Since Hook had a forty-one-year-old daughter, he couldn't imagine if he and Susan had lost her at birth. Life would be totally different and disappointing. "See you later."

He called his Atlanta private detective, Ms. Monaco. "Sydney, it's Hook. Hear me out. You're a busy private eye, but I need you. Can you come by the cafeteria at five o'clock today? Fill me in on any news you've acquired about our investigation and, also, another one of my machines was stolen before it made it to the lab."

"I can and will meet you. Where, when, and how did this theft take place?"

"Earlier today at the back of the campus—in the parking lot, from a van, before being handed off to the loading dock's personnel. An infant from the newborn nursery went missing at the same time, and there was an above-normal police presence in the area."

The hair on her skin bristled with anger. "I'm a physician before I'm a P.I., and that baby's health and life could be in danger."

"Tell me about it."

"Say no more. I'll be there."

They both hung up, but Sydney decided to set new priorities for the rest of the day.

Cynthia and Alex peeked around the aisle, aware that Hook would be leaving for his five o'clock meeting. His head was bent over a round lab dish, and a pipette hung between his index finger and thumb.

"Dr. Hookie, it's almost time to leave for the day, but Alex and I were wondering if we could tag along to your meeting."

"You are welcome to come" he said, giving his loyal workers a glance, "but I think a romantic dinner in a fine restaurant would be far more enjoyable for the two of you."

"Dr. Hookie," she replied, "you hired us because of our nerdy characteristics and our dogged determination with double-stranded

DNA—not because we run amok at five o'clock each day and go to bars, restaurants, or casinos."

"You two are impossible. Suit yourself."

With the youngsters help, they put away research materials into the refrigerators, and Hook hung up his white coat. He pitched his second root beer can into the garbage, and they turned out the lights.

"I hate that I need to do this," Hook said, locking the lab door behind them. "Yet this flimsy lock method isn't going to stop anyone if they have their mind set on breaking in."

"So true," Alex added. "I wish they would install security cameras in the hallway."

They headed towards the elevator, and Hook pressed the down button. "Think about it, however. What a tremendous cost that would be if the campus installed cameras in every hallway, every main office, every lobby. And who would monitor all that? To incur those changes, a bigger security bill would somehow be factored into folks' medical bills. Cost prohibitive in my opinion."

The elevator went to ground and the three colleagues peeled off to the cafeteria and chose a place to sit. Freddie Simpson came out of nowhere and stood over their table. "Can I buy anyone a drink?"

"Cynthia and Alex could use a romantic bottle of wine, but instead, they're by my side, the ever loyal employees."

"Wine from the best vineyards is beyond my pocket change these days, but I'll spring for a soft drink."

They shook their heads, and Freddie pulled out a chair.

"Here she comes," Hook said.

Sydney Monaco arrived, straightened her slender build, and directed her glance at Hook. "Dr. Hookie, always a pleasure to see you and your colleagues. Since you called me today, I redirected my energies to this new development. Let's go, unless you and your group are going to feed your faces."

Hook popped up and gave his right lower leg a quick massage as if awakening it from a nap. No one questioned Sydney, and they followed her like pups in a litter. She turned her head to Freddie.

"What is this I heard about a stolen infant?"

"The baby was in the newborn nursery. Born a few hours earlier, medically cleared, and wrapped and snugly in a bassinet. Nurses go in and out of there regularly, and there had been intermittent visitors at the window for all the infants. Anyway, for a short time, no one was at the window, and the nurses were all busy in the other room. No one in there for a short period is not uncommon, and not a problem. But it was this morning. A visitor called in, asking where the baby was, because it wasn't with the mother in her room."

"Hell, that's terrible."

"Where are we going?" Hook asked.

"To show you security camera footage, which I combed through for the last two hours."

They passed the Campus Coffee and Bakery Shop, and Sydney led them up the staircase of the doctor's office building. They made a right on the second floor, and she opened the door to the central station for all security monitoring on the campus.

Hook had never set foot in the department. At first, three spacey partitioned areas housed enough live security footage to keep a dozen people busy, but those three regions opened up into a bigger zone running horizontally from wall to wall.

The group ended near the back wall where a middle- aged man rolled his chair to allow them to move closer. "Ms. Monaco, help yourself."

"This is Dr. Hookie and his crew," she said. "And, of course, you know Mr. Simpson." She glanced at Hook. "I made friends in here today, along with Atlanta police officers who were evaluating camera footage."

The man titled his head. "I've worked here for twelve years, and we've never seen such a police presence in here before. You'd think everyone walked in to draw a winning sweepstakes ticket."

Sydney shot him a small smile, and waved her group to a cluster of monitors and began pushing buttons. Her tone became serious. "We're dealing with professionals, or someone who learned the theft trade fast and furious, and has luck on their side. With today's caper, the serendipity they encountered was a windfall. All the focus centered on a kidnapping."

She scanned to a particular spot and stopped the footage. "What we're going to see is prior to the time the delivery men realized their big box was gone. I evaluated these films multiple times, paying strict attention to each entrance and exit from the back of the campus, as well as what I can dig up from the parking lot."

Sydney pushed the forward arrow and the footage began. "This is looking down from a camera outside the ER, mounted to the right."

An old woman with a cane, holding onto a man with her free hand, ambled out the door. At least a minute passed, the automatic doors opened again, and a paramedic walked outside, nothing in his arms. Two women in scrubs passed through, talking feverishly, only with small purses in their possession.

"As you can see, no one here had the infant, nor do they look like they are going to start a robbery."

"But you still can't be sure, can you?" Alex asked.

"Correct. However, I did check on the employment status of the paramedic, and he is legit. Soon Freddie steps out."

They waited for their security guard to appear as the doors slid open and a woman came out. Her shoulder-length hair was blonde with a faint impression of darker roots. Tall and slender, she sported a fine figure. She wore blue jeans and a yellow blouse, the top buttons undone. In her hands was a cell phone and a slender shoulder bag hung by her side.

In an apparent hurry, Freddie appeared next and bumped into her.

"Ouch," Hook said, watching the woman pop her hand to her head and press down. "You clunked right into her."

"I sure felt bad about that."

Everyone's eyes stayed on the screen. "What did you say to her?" Sydney asked.

"I asked her if anyone had come out of those doors holding an infant. She said no, and that is when the police cars showed up."

On the monitor, Freddie walked off, and subsequently the blonde did too. The group continued to watch, as a few onlookers showed up gawking at the parking lot—which had become the focus of a police presence.

Sydney switched to the adjacent monitor and her onlookers moved over. She pulled up the loading dock footage from earlier in the day, the area where the actual heist took place.

CHAPTER 9

Hook, Cynthia, Alex, and Freddie Simpson hovered over Sydney's shoulder as the monitor streamed footage from above the loading dock. Campus men did heavy lifting off a dolly stacked with large boxes while Freddie appeared on the platform. Two men with work uniforms showed up and spoke to him.

"What did they say to you?" Sydney asked.

"They were the delivery truck guys telling me an item went missing from the back of their truck. I'm so sorry I didn't pay more attention, because later I realized it was Dr. Hookie's item."

"Don't worry about the machine," Hook said, "the baby was the priority."

They continued to watch, and then Sydney backed the film up to cover a greater amount of time before the heist. Aggravated, she shook her head. "This camera doesn't catch deeper into the lot."

Sydney switched to another camera's footage. "This catches the back of the parking lot, but the view is angled across the lot for the cars only turning in or going straight out. And, how stupid, it doesn't catch license plates and you can barely make out car makes and models."

"So where do we stand?" Hook asked.

Sydney turned around and semi-sat on the end of the counter. "I wanted to show you all this material to drive home the idea that I'm coming up short on this perp. They know where the cameras are, and they know what they're doing. Plus, today they may have had extra luck."

Hook sighed, and narrowed his eyes. "What now?"

"Besides looking at the front end of these heists, today I started focusing on the back end of these scenarios. Why is this equipment being stolen? Obviously to sell—either to customers in need of medical equipment who don't know that it was robbed, or to people or facilities who are aware that it is stolen goods."

Freddie laughed. "That narrows it down."

"Ha, I wish. Anyway, although I'm checking as thoroughly as I can, I doubt if the equipment is staying in the Atlanta area. A smart thief would not take the chance.

"My online search for medical equipment has begun—anything at all that smacks of stolen equipment. And, more importantly, I have contacts all over the United States, and my contacts have contacts. The buying and selling of medical equipment is a priority on my radar and my contacts will serve me faithfully as well." She glanced at Hook. "And Next Generation Sequencing Machines are not an everyday item, so we'll get these smart alecks sooner or later."

Hook turned his head back to the monitor, his silver-haired ponytail in everyone's view. "Thanks, Sydney, and thanks to you too, Freddie. Capers aren't solved overnight, especially one that takes a backseat to a missing infant."

Glimpsing at Cynthia and Alex, he said, "Good night, you two. See you in the morning."

The group broke up, Hook stopped at the grocery store for fresh ingredients for dinner, and set off for home.

Hook twiddled his thumbs over the selection of fish in the frozen food section. The slot with jumbo shrimp was empty, so he selected a bag of medium shrimp. He passed the produce section and snatched a pound of fresh brussel sprouts.

At home, Hook eased the door open and Bentley curved around from behind to greet him. "Hello beast. Are you being a fine fellow today?"

The attentive cat walked beside him to the kitchen, and he unloaded the small market bag. Susan showed up from the laundry room with a neat pile of folded laundry in her arms.

"Hi honey," he said. "How was your day?"

"Quiet and peaceful, just the way I like it."

"No major catastrophes. Wonderful."

"I can read you like a book, which means a catastrophe happened at work."

"You are so clever. Maybe so."

"Plus, you are later than normal." She set the clothes down and reached for a half-full glass of diet soda.

"I'll fill you in over dinner. Today's the day you usually check your sugar. Did you?" He pulled out a frying pan, and then set down Bentley's bowl with more water.

"I'm running around one-hundred-ten these days. Your cooking has a lot to do with it."

"The noodles we're having tonight don't help, but everything in moderation, so I say." Hook stir-fried shrimp with a light Thai sauce and boiled noodles while Susan cut the stems off the vegetables. He soon placed them in the oven to roast.

With cooking finished, and food scooped on their plates, Hook sat down with his wife and added salt to the vegetables. He grimaced, not wanting to tell his wife what would bother her more than what happened earlier to him. "An infant was snatched from the newborn nursery today, taken away from his or her mother who is still in the hospital."

Susan gasped. "How could that happen? Or, who would do such a thing?"

He shook his head slowly. "Honey, I can't answer your questions, except that whoever did such a thing is a monster."

"Please tell me when they find that baby, so I can rest my mind for the child as well as for the mother."

"Sure. We'll add them to our prayers." He chewed a shrimp and put down his fork. Even though his life revolved around science, he supported his wife's religious beliefs, and held onto some of his own as well.

"However, another one of my machines was stolen today from the premises, before it made it upstairs."

"What a shame. What are you going to do?"

"Sydney Monaco is helping out, and was more pro-active today."

Susan's amber eyes glanced at Bentley who stared up at her with a forlorn expression. "How do thieves go about pulling something like that off, unless it was what they call an 'inside' job?"

"Since I'm not a thief, I can't think like one."

Eating faster than Hook, Susan became quiet, and he traced his mind back to the security videos he'd watched earlier. He replayed them several times. Over the years, he had learned, by going over something multiple times in his mind right away, he could retain the information like having a photographic memory.

"I'll start washing the dishes," Susan said, when she'd finished. "Especially since you're such a slow poke tonight."

"That's fine. I suppose I'm not very hungry."

"Must be, because the food served in this establishment is always the best." She rose, and gave him a kiss on his forehead.

After dinner, Hook sat in his leather recliner with Bentley. The cat molded into his lap, Hook's hands stroking until his head nodded off in a gentle slumber.

An hour after the heist, Belinda called Duane. "Meet me at the house," she said, and hung up.

Her meaning was clear to him, because her two-car garage was where they stashed their goods before shipping anything off to Linda and Dirk in Chicago. Her surroundings qualified as a transient area, barely a middle-income neighborhood. The homes were neatly kept by most homeowners and the area was safe, as well as off the radar from any police patrols or scrutiny.

She stood by the front window, the blinds cracked, waiting for him to arrive, and called Linda.

"Hey," Linda said after taking the call.

"Boy, do I have a surprise. Another one of those expensive genetic testing machines."

Linda felt a surge of adrenaline, and careful not to say anything too blatant on the phone, she said, "Outstanding of you to sniff out work for us again so soon. When is the purchase?"

"Already completed."

Linda pumped a fist in the air, and decided to give her sister some credit. "Right from birth, you're always a few minutes ahead of me."

"Cut yourself some slack. We're in this fifty-fifty. Plus, look at it this way. You're younger than me and that will never change. I'll always be an old person compared to you."

Linda smiled. They revisited this type of conversation every so often and it was part of their bond. "Which means you'll have dementia before me, so I better watch out for our business interests as carefully as you do, uhh—the items we sometimes acquire."

"I don't mind. By the way, did I mention? Art work may be in our near future."

"What kind of disposal are you considering?"

"I was thinking of using an online auction, or sending it your way—if the materials in question materialize."

"Hmm. Okay. Keep me posted."

"Yes, and Duane just drove in. Talk later."

Belinda walked over to the inside garage door, stepped out, and hit the switch to the empty side. Duane slithered under the door as it opened, his square chin sticking forward, success plastered all over his face.

"That was frigging awesome," he said. "Right under their noses, cops all over the place, and the 'man' did it." He jerked his arm up and flexed his biceps.

"I'll give you credit, Duane, but we *both* pulled it off with a diversion which we didn't count on, which was very risky."

"The cops even stopped me. Damn. I was meant for this business."

"All right, congratulations to both of us. Another big ticket item under our belt. Let's move her into the garage."

"Safer if I move my vehicle in here, and then we unload."

"At least you're thinking clearly despite your inflated brain."

He shot her a distorted facial expression of disapproval, turned and hurried out. After pulling the gray van in, they closed the door, opened the back, and moved the NGS machine to a bottom shelf, already lined with several items for transport to Linda and Dirk.

Waving him in the house, Belinda said, "Because the opportunity is going to present itself, we *are* temporarily going into the art business."

"I prefer if the pictures were a Picasso or something."

"I wish, but they are valuable enough for the hospital to hang in their main lobbies, and probably easy enough to snatch and sell off on the internet art auctions I mentioned before. I need to do some more snooping around."

"When is this happening?"

"Before some kind of health fair they are sponsoring."

"A campus wide health fair?"

"I suppose so."

"Ha! Like I mentioned, perhaps I can get my blood pressure checked."

"Fat chance. Don't get sloppy."

Belinda reached into the refrigerator, pulled out a block of cheese, and handed him a beer. She cut some slices of cheese, and dumped some crackers out of a box.

"We don't have to eat," he said. He inched his eyebrows up and gave her a lopsided smile. "We're the same age, the same empty marital status, and partners in crime. Two people can't be closer than that."

"Except if we were family members," she responded, not being surprised at his sexual suggestion. His attempts to court her came up once in awhile, but not enough for her to be annoyed with him.

"In my opinion, that's disgusting. Isn't that incest?"

She savored a cranberry infused piece of cheese and nodded.

Duane sighed. "Okay, then I'm out of here. Today you're driving me crazy. I like that look you're wearing."

"No problem. Enjoy the beer. Call you by tomorrow."

He flicked the beer cap into the garbage and left.

In the bedroom, Hook picked Bentley up and gave him a squeeze while his wife slept comfortably. He dressed quietly and headed out, earlier than usual without putting on a pot of coffee.

At the Campus Coffee and Bakery Shop there was no line, but he wavered over what to order.

"Dr. Hookie, can't make up your mind today?" the barista asked.

"I'll change that. How about a dark roast Americano?"

"Sure thing."

Stepping over to the bulletin board, he noticed the first flyer tacked up announcing the health fair. That was another issue he needed to address, he thought, as he reached back over for his coffee.

Upstairs in the lab, he flipped the light switch on, and went through his overdue mail pile from the day before as he sipped the strong brew.

As promised, Kent Wadsworth had sent him an interoffice memo about the upcoming campus event. Please give me the details, it said, about your demonstration for the health fair.

People don't understand the complexity of what a genetic lab does, he thought. A demonstration would be fine, but hardly likely. Better to give away something for free. He leaned back and pondered. A total DNA genetic analysis, like the one he had recently performed for Karissa Larson, would be a windfall for someone.

A complete DNA analysis that someone could win would draw attention to what the lab does, and what it is capable of. But more importantly, it would alert customers to the fact that the testing is as simple as a blood or saliva test and it can answer important questions about their risk for certain cancers. The testing, in his opinion, is the most important information that people can ever receive about their future health.

"Good morning," Alex said, poking his head in. "Thanks for letting us partake in that discussion with your private investigator last night."

"No problem. Did the two of you grab a nice dinner?"

Alex laughed. "Not exactly. We both went to the gym."

"That'll do. A couple that works out together stays together."

"I'll remember that."

"What do you think if I offer a free DNA analysis for our participation in the health fair?"

"Sounds remarkable, but we'll need a new NGS machine before making that promise."

Hook laughed. "Excellent point. What better way for us to receive a cash advancement or full payment for the equipment if it is needed to perform our giveaway prize."

"There you go."

Alex walked back into the lab and Hook picked up the phone to call the hospital's Associate Executive Director. "Kent, it's Hook Hookie here. I just read your memo, and rather than your suggestion of a demonstration by my department, maybe we can offer a full fledged DNA analysis for a lucky winner."

Kent swiveled around in his chair to glance out the window. "That would be sorely appreciated, as well as a fantastic contribution."

"Only thing is, the genetic testing machine being delivered yesterday was stolen. Someone in Atlanta is running a market on expensive NGS machines, jeopardizing genetic pathologists' work like mine."

"So I heard, Dr. Hookie. I'm so sorry about this."

"Can the hospital cut through the red tape on this one and get me a machine ASAP?"

Kent took a minute to consider, but he had no choice. Dr. Hookie must have also been a car salesman in the past. "Because I can lump this into the cost of the health fair, I believe so. Otherwise, I doubt if the hospital could cough up money again so soon under 'medical equipment.'"

"Stellar," Hook said. He hung up quickly before the hospital director changed his mind.

CHAPTER 10

"Stack those tables against the wall." A lanky worker wearing a faded brown baseball cap pointed to the left side of the hospital lobby, and two men started removing a pile of collapsible tables from a dolly. It was 8 a.m. Monday morning, and the health fair preparation had begun.

The wiry man in charge of the preliminary setup, Bruce, walked away to survey the lobbies of the doctors' office building and hospital as well as the hallway between them on either side of the Campus Coffee and Bakery Shop. His instructions from Kent Wadsworth were clear—put equipment out of the way against the walls, cover any of it with drop clothss so as not to be an eyesore to patients and visitors, and make sure none of it poses a safety hazard.

The rich aroma of coffee pulled him into the coffee shop, and he stepped up to the empty counter. "Black, make it black as tar, and in your largest cup."

"From the pot or do you want an Americano or espresso?"

"Okay, use your skills and make me a whopper."

The barista never heard a cup of coffee be called a hamburger before, but she turned and cranked out an Americano with a double shot of espresso. Bruce paid and sat at the table closest to the door.

Belinda, on her way to an appointment, noticed the man veer in from the hallway, and also heeded her urge for coffee. She jumped around with her order all the time and was as unreliable in her coffee order as non dependable employees. Since she wasn't fussy about how her java was served—it was all palatable—she varied her orders on purpose for a reason.

She ordered a vanilla cappuccino and asked for a blueberry scone. After paying, she carefully selected her table, and placed down her items. A few people dotted the tables, but they either drank their coffee or scrolled around on their cell phones. She leaned over and broke the silence.

Although she suspected the answer to her question, she nevertheless elicited a conversation with Bruce. "You and your men in the lobby—is your work related to the event the hospital is hosting at the end of the week?"

She's pretty, Bruce thought. At thirty-two years old, he was engaged for the first time, but rarely did women talk to him out of the blue. "Yes. I'm to be sure that..." he started, but wanted to correct his English. "Friday will be a big deal. I am in charge of the entire setup, which is important. The fair will be educational for many people, and I'll be doing my part to help patients get some kind of health intervention." He frowned. That came out a lot more wordy than he wanted. But did he care? He was engaged, and she was too cute not to have a boyfriend.

"Yes. There is the possibility that some good will come of it. People walk around with undiagnosed hypertension and diabetes all the time."

"You must be in medicine."

"No, I'm not on the provider side of medicine. They still plan on hosting the event on Friday, is that correct?" She crossed her legs while he nodded. "Then you must be booked for the whole week."

"Yes, we are, and there is more to it than meets the eye."

"But what about the stuff you leave out until then? I would assume some of it is expensive."

"Each vendor will bring his or her own equipment Thursday night or at the crack of dawn on Friday. They'll set up then. At the last minute, security and the hospital won't worry about the tables because many of the vendors will be lurking about. And we'll be draping over the items we place ahead of time. We'll be changing some lobbies, too, sprucing up the bland pictures with new art work. The Associate Executive Director put a bunch of money into the campus's face lift and health fair."

Feeling important with all the inside-knowledge he told her, he smiled.

"Guess I'll pass by you in the hospital lobby."

"I'll mostly be on that side today and tomorrow. Wednesday I'll start the hallway, and Thursday the lobby in the doctor's building." He hoped she would choose to have another encounter with him. "What's your name?"

Unflappable, and making one up, she said, "Becky. What's yours?"

"Bruce."

"Do you need more help from the hospital? Are the art pieces large?" She knew she was now asking a lot of questions, but it didn't matter. Next time on campus, this Bruce wouldn't recognize her, even if she sat on his lap.

He grasped the bottom rim of his chair, scooted in, and lessened the distance between them.

"There's another guy with me, but the paintings or prints, or whatever they are, are easily handled by me alone. The only teamwork needed will be putting the hooks in the right place, and hanging them straight. Actually…" He leaned in further. "The smallest ones are the most expensive. I know because I accepted the bill on delivery."

"I'm relieved. Sounds easy and safe enough for you. It was wonderful to meet you." She wrapped the other half of her scone in a napkin, and picked up her to-go cup. "I better get going."

"Me too," he said, and jumped up. The rich aromatic steam of his coffee faded as he followed her out, parted direction, and strolled to the hospital lobby.

Belinda focused on the outside view through the window panes, stifling her enthusiasm. Some people are so dumb, she thought, especially men.

As she took in the billowy clouds puffing across the top of the medical school across the way, she wished she'd had the opportunity to become a doctor. She was smart enough. Too bad her brainpower was being used to hurt medical care rather than help it.

Cynthia and Alex walked quickly along the hallway, headed to the elevator, and upstairs to work. They scooted to the right to pass Belinda, and Cynthia noted the woman's unusual walk. Her sister had done the same thing when she was young—toed in with one foot—but she had grown out of it in her teenage years. This poor woman they passed still carried the affliction.

Alex pressed the elevator button and they rode in silence. "Let's lift Dr. Hookie's spirits today," Cynthia said as they stepped out.

"Our presence always does that," Alex kidded her. "We're half his age and more."

"Just because we're younger, doesn't mean squat. He is the humblest, most self-confident, balanced, and intelligent man I know. I'm just saying. Let's give him a smile or two today. This problem with his machine is weighing him down because it is extra work he doesn't need. His gray matter should be spent on more productive tasks."

Alex squeezed her arm. "That is one reason why I think I love you.

You're so thoughtful of others."

She stopped short before their bench. "What did you just say?"

"I half-said I love you."

"Well... Do you or don't you?" she grinned.

He glanced up and down the aisle. Hook was not around, so he leaned in and kissed her. More than planting a quick one on her lips, he lingered, and put his hand in the small of her back.

Hook turned the corner by the windows, caught them in the act, and cleared his throat.

"Oops," Cynthia said. "Sorry, Dr. Hookie. This is a workplace, yet I'll vouch for the kiss being important at this time."

He raised an eyebrow and kept approaching them. "I'll take you at your word—this time."

"She's right," Alex said, "but I'll mind my manners. Is there anything extra important on our agenda this week? Anything we can specifically do for you?"

"Sure. Which is why I'm here. Come on, let's go in the office."

Alex and Cynthia settled in the two available chairs in front of his desk as he reached into the refrigerator and took out a root beer soda. "I don't want to chase down my coffee just yet, but this drink can warm up a bit. I hate freezing cold drinks." He sat and rolled the chair back towards the window.

"I have good news," he added, the smile lines creasing at the end of his eyes. "Kent Wadsworth, in charge of Friday's health event, is lumping the cost of our next NGS machine into the cost of the fair. Which means we're getting it ASAP. I popped him a call already, and my item is coming straight from the company by special delivery. When it arrives tomorrow, I'm personally going out to the truck and bringing it up here myself! And none of this back-door delivery either. I told Kent to make the trucker pull up in the front of the hospital." He jutted his chin towards Alex. "Since my joints need more tender loving care than yours do, maybe you can lend me a hand when the time is right."

"No problem, Dr. Hookie. But how is he budgeting the machine into the fair?"

"I'm going to give away a full free DNA genetic analysis. Like a raffle drawing. I can't promise comprehensive testing if I don't have both the Illumina and the Microarray machines." He smiled.

"See, that was easy," Cynthia said, tapping Alex on the hand.

"What was easy?" Hook asked.

"To get you to smile today at work," she said.

"Well, sure, with a new machine imminent, why wouldn't I?"

"You're married to your work." Alex shook his head.

"No. I'm married to my wife, and engaged permanently to my work."

"That's the epitome of any long-term relationship if you ask me," Cynthia said.

"Most marriages don't come close. Anyway, I've decided. At least two of us can kiss the lab good-bye on Friday to take the day off from here. It will take team work to educate the public, run the table, and take bathroom and food breaks. Is that acceptable?"

"I'm in," Cynthia said.

"I'll second what she said," Alex chimed in.

"Good." Already antsy to get up, he rose from the chair. "Off you go, and save your kissing for tonight."

Early in the evening, Duane Harper was exhausted as he pulled into Belinda's driveway and rapped his knuckles on the front door. She swung open the fading brown door and ushered him in.

"I'm wiped," he said.

"How'd the drive back go?" she asked, and promptly went to the refrigerator and pulled him out a beer.

Duane sucked in a breath and eyed what she was wearing—thin leggings shaped her fine legs, and a pink, long top draped over her waistline.

"I'm beginning to think I can do this Atlanta to Chicago drive in my sleep. But it's grueling, and I'm no truck driver." He had left late Friday and, except for conducting business with Linda Sisko and Dirk Crouch and staying overnight in hotels, he'd been on the road.

"I would imagine that between the two cities, the drive is a piece of cake—free time to listen to audio books or get fired up about political rhetoric on the radio."

He gulped down some cold brew and set down the can. "Why don't you come with me sometime and see your sister?"

"Someone needs to do the groundwork here or there'll be nothing to haul off to Chicago! I befriended some schmuck worker this morning, so we have work to do tomorrow."

"And I thought I was going to sleep in tomorrow. Hey, I could always stay here, saving me from going back and forth. We could even sleep in the same bed."

"No." She grimaced and held back showing any emotion. "I know you mean well, and I'm flattered, but you wouldn't like what you find."

He inched his hand over to touch her, but she withdrew.

"Back to business. Thanks for keeping me posted with the drop-off in Chicago. We couldn't have a better set-up."

"Your sister already has a buyer for that genetic testing machine we just stole."

"There is high demand these days for high-end, high-tech machines, and there are more wizard scientists doing analyses."

"And the prices for the equipment make me salivate."

"However, what happens is that over time, as newer updates to the equipment comes out, the price of the older models drops significantly, which is another reason we need to unload the stuff quickly for the best deal."

"Plus, it's hot as hell. Don't forget that. Who knows what kind of security changes the campus is making, or how many cops are working on our robberies."

"That is why we must recheck the cameras in front of the hospital early tomorrow morning. Then, I'm going to execute an art theft from the lobby. You are going to be posted this time in the center of the parking lot out front, where I believe there is no camera coverage."

Duane cocked his head. "How are you going to carry artwork?"

"First, the pieces are in boxes, and I learned that apparently the height and width are manageable. I want your pants and shirt, the set you use when you imitate a hospital worker, even the belt. And bring me a baseball cap. Not that bright orange one you wear, but do you own a brown one, slightly faded? I need to mimic the guy I talked with today.

"Sure. I own a stash of hats. But will my clothes be too big on you?"

"No way. They are going to fit me like a glove."

Duane chucked down the rest of his beer and smacked his lips.

"One more thing. Let's go sweep out and tidy up the back of the truck

68

for this job—in case a box were to open up, we don't want the canvases getting dirty or damaged in any way." She signaled to the inside garage door, which meant she wanted him to pull in the vehicle.

He shook his head. She was so damn methodical, the brain child of their operations, she thought of everything. Although he felt like a Mack truck had run over him, he did what she asked.

CHAPTER 11

As soon as Hook opened the garage door to the house, Bentley weaved around his legs with a purr. "Yes, it's me, and you are the best cat watchdog that exists."

The cat slunk away into the kitchen, and Hook found Susan wiping the counter with a dishcloth. He sidled next to her and kissed her cheek. "How was your day, dear?"

"Just fine, except for those veins popping up in my legs. My calves are aching and the bottom of my feet tingle."

"Your diabetes needs to leave your feet alone. How about I give them a little massage tonight? Make your blood flow down there and warm them up."

Her eyes widened, the delight showing on her face, which was a rare thing. "Gratefully, I will take you up on your offer."

"And what are you doing here?"

The portable grill and two unopened cheese packages sat at the end of the counter, and she grabbed a package of bread by the sink.

"Making us dinner tonight—grilled cheese sandwiches on the grill—they will be the best with the cheese hot and runny."

"Excellent. While you do that, I'll make us a big bowl of salad."

She plugged the grill in while Hook delivered on the tossed greens.

"How was your day?" she asked.

"Cynthia and Alex seem to be ramping up their relationship. Better that way than having two lab techs who don't get along and work under my roof."

"Hmm. If we ever are invited to their wedding, I'll do my best to attend."

"Young people don't jump into marriages these days like us old folks used to do, partly because society doesn't crucify them anymore for living together in 'sin.' This way, I believe, is much better. Their divorce rate down the road may be a lot less."

"Why do you think that?"

"Because they have more time to see each other's faults and make a rational decision about committing to 'death do us part.'"

"Would you have married me if we had had a long engagement and you learned that I was a troubled, introverted individual?"

Not wanting to delay thinking about the answer, he said, "Dear, a long betrothal would not have changed a thing. We were meant to be together for eternity."

"That's a long time."

"Certainly. Before and after death."

They continued in silence, as he mulled over what she had admitted. She had never before muttered such words to him before—what he already knew—a truthful description of her personality.

After assembling a layer of cheese on the bread, she placed the sandwiches between the upper and lower parts of the grill.

"The hospital arranged for the delivery of another genetic analysis machine for me tomorrow. The purchase is semi-dependent on my participation in the health and fitness fair on Friday."

"That was kind of them. You can't do your work without all that intelligent machinery, I'm sure."

"If you want to step out of the house at the end of the week, you may enjoy coming by."

She gave him a tilt of her head and opened the grill, but the sandwiches weren't done yet.

"We can leave them there another minute or two," he said. "Let the cheese melt like butter into the bread. In the meantime, let's dish out some of this salad."

Although he was thin as a straw, Bruce puffed his chest out with importance. Kent Wadsworth had officially appointed him in charge of the health fair set up, and he'd learned that meant a few extra dollars in salary. He carried his insulated coffee mug around which he had brought from home, and placed it down on the reception desk in the hospital lobby.

"Good morning Lou Anne," he said to the elderly woman wearing a coral-colored volunteer jacket with a name tag.

"Guess you'll be spending a lot of time here this week. What's your name?" Her hair was the same color as her dentures, and she gave him a pleasant smile.

"Bruce. You, and Freddie Simpson, and me and my men have the entire responsibility of making Friday's event run smoothly. By getting the prep work done efficiently, by making people feel welcome, and making the lobby look like the entrance to a five-star hotel, we are doing a humongous service."

"Never thought of it in those terms."

"Sure enough. People up top may make the decisions, but they are worthless unless the important people do the work. And look at you, you work for free!"

The smile lines around her eyes flickered. "Even though I stand behind this counter, let me know how I can help today."

"You can start by minding my coffee cup before I need to refill it." He left the container and unhinged one of the white tables. After setting it up facing the middle of the lobby and along the line of the entrance, he did the same thing on the other side. He pulled out tablecloths from a box in the corner, and set them on both tables, then put two folding chairs behind each of them.

Bruce grabbed his coffee and stood with another worker against the wall as Freddie Simpson strolled through.

"I see y'all are being the early birds you're supposed to be," Freddie said. "I am as excited about Friday as everyone else. I'm going to make use of some services myself."

"Those two tables I just set out," Bruce said, "will be staffed by hospital employees who will register those wanting to come, but patients can still 'walk in' without being listed."

"I'll wait then, and slip in for free services on Friday when I can."

"Perfect. I'll be doing the same thing."

"Looks like Kent Wadsworth himself is setting up a registration table," Freddie said. "I'm going to the doctor's building where I will be more needed. This place is swarming with keen eyes."

"That's a fact. Actually, we'll follow you. I need to put out registration tables in their lobby as well."

They took off while Kent unpacked supplies on the table facing the right. A woman was with him, and two women crossed to the other table with their own box.

Kent placed laminated signs inside plastic stands and set them out. They were chock-full of information:

Monument Medical Center Presents a
HEALTH AND FITNESS FAIR

Our medical center wants our community to be healthy. Join us for our bi-annual Health and Fitness Fair. This Friday, take part in health screenings offered at affordable prices or for free.
Blood Pressure Free
Oxygen saturation Free
Bone Density $10
Complete Blood Count $10
Pulmonary Function Test $10
Hemoglobin A1C $15

The list went on with more tests and their prices, and then finished with the following:

Complete DNA analysis for high-risk cancers $145
Complete Vascular Package $145

And ... there will be two free raffle drawings! One for a FREE DNA analysis and one for a FREE Complete Vascular Package. Stop by the tables to learn more.
And be sure to visit our INFORMATION BOOTHS as well!

Since eight o'clock in the morning, Belinda had moved around upstairs on the second floor balcony. From sitting at one of the few round tables, to walking across the length of the upstairs lobby, or now standing still overlooking the first floor, she had the presence and position of the employees memorized.

Meanwhile, Duane hung out in their gray van parked smack in the middle of the front parking lot. No way were any security cameras picking him up. He guessed the hospital only thought about, and focused on, the entrance where people went in and out, as well as vehicles exiting to the main street. They could even skirt that street camera, he knew, by weaving over to the lane going out to the side street. And they were avoiding the back of the hospital where they had been the previous week.

He grabbed his black coffee from the cup holder and sipped. Music streamed on his iPhone, but he kept the volume low since the window was cracked, and he wanted to draw no attention. Most of the real activity regarding patients did not occur in the lot, but at the circular drop-off at the hospital's front door. Family or friends of patients unloaded wheel chairs and walkers from vehicles, and assisted them to the lobby and then parked their cars.

Duane had the easy part of this heist. Belinda was doing the heavy lifting, maybe even literally. However, he was ready to meet her between the vehicle and some safe distance from the entrance if she came out with what looked like a too-heavy box.

His partner, confident the coast was clear, avoided the elevator, and walked down the curved staircase, her eyes glued on the large space. Her black shoes were soft and quiet, and Duane's clothes fit her perfectly, and matched the color and work style of the workers. As importantly, the faded brown baseball cap that she wore on her head, that Duane had lent her, mimicked Bruce's to a tee.

With her head pointed more to the ground than straight ahead, she walked to the side wall where boxes were intermittently leaning between the folded white tables which were not set up.

There would be no dilly-dallying, she thought, as she removed a box cutter from her pocket and flicked it open. It was imperative that she check the inside of the cardboard containers to make sure the contents held an oil painting canvas, or framed canvas, or a glass-framed watercolor, or something similar.

She slid the cutter across the tape along the top edge and managed to peek inside. A picture was inside, and she could make out its bright colors. The cutter went back into her trousers. Since the box's height stood between her hip and knee, she decided to take it as a solo, and tightened her hands around the manageable width.

Straight out the door she went like she had just selected and paid for a product in a fancy department store. At the van, Duane slipped out of the vehicle, and opened the back door. She left it to him, they did not speak, and she went straight back into the lobby.

Two women crossed the rubber mat behind Belinda and, curious about the presentation in the lobby, stopped in front of Kent's table. As he greeted them, he glanced at the other person who also came in, and was pleased that Bruce was working the lobby, because that meant that all the pictures should be up on the wall by the end of the day.

"Ladies," Kent said, "don't leave it to chance that you will be back on Friday. Please make an appointment here to find out your Vitamin D level, or B-12 level, or have other lab work drawn at the end of the week. And you will have stupendous odds for winning one of our raffle prizes if you enter the drawings."

The two women placed their signatures in a time slot on the clipboard. "Thank you so much," the first woman said. "We'll be back."

Kent smiled as they walked on to the reception desk. The morning gave him a respite from administrative duties and a chance to mingle with the folks that walked into their facility. He took a look again at the huge sculpture in the foyer which he loved, a big expense which he had approved four years ago.

Although Kent could not see his face, skinny Bruce walked in front of the statue again, this time holding two cardboard boxes. They were the type sitting against the walls with the art work, but Kent figured he was busing empty boxes out to one of the dumpsters. His workers knew what they were doing, and he could depend on them.

"Who wants to come with me?" Dr. Hookie asked. He wore a sly smile, happy about something, as Cynthia moved a lab tray out of the refrigerator and Alex spun vials in a machine.

"Where to?" she asked.

"The front of the hospital. I'm signing for the delivery of our replacement sequencing machine."

"Get out!" Alex exclaimed. "Let's go."

"We can be your bodyguards," Cynthia said.

"And I'll treat us to a cup of caffeine." Hook hung his lab coat on the coat rack, and they single filed out the door. The elevator landed on ground, and they made a left past the coffee shop.

"Dr. Hookie," Cynthia said, "you aren't a spring chicken and Alex is no bulked-up weightlifter. Using a dolly would be a lot easier to transport the machine."

"My wife is an introvert and rarely offers me suggestions about how to do things." He rolled his eyes. "I sometimes forget the way most women offer advice when men don't want to hear it."

"Sorry, Dr. Hookie."

"No reason to be sorry. You are correct, of course."

Making it into the huge space of the lobby, Hook made a dead stop as he glanced to the left. A lean worker wearing a worn, brown baseball cap was peeking inside a carton against the wall.

"Excuse me. I'm Dr. Hookie and I work at the top floor of the doctor's building. With the fair preparations going on, do you happen to have a dolly that I can borrow for a few minutes? I need to transport a box upstairs." From the side, the man lifted his head only slightly.

Belinda froze when the man came over, and her heart practically exploded out of her chest when he said "Dr. Hookie." She gulped, and thought quickly. Not wanting to use her own voice, she acted like something caught in her throat, and coughed. She pointed to the corner by some stacked tables, inviting him to use the rolling platform next to them.

"Thanks," he said and took a step. "I'll bring it back in about twenty minutes. My wonder machine is here!"

"He's like a father with a newborn," Cynthia chimed in towards Belinda, "wanting to give out cigars. That's how much his equipment means to him."

Belinda nodded while, luckily, Cynthia and Alex decided to follow Hook, but there were too many tables in the way, and they decided not to use the rolling device.

The box leaning against Belinda's leg possessed what looked like an oil painting of a seashore. What a fine addition to the lobby, she thought, although it would never hang here. She hurried, especially since Duane was twiddling his thumbs at the truck. He could be careless when left idle.

She beat Hook, Cynthia, and Alex, and walked out with the box as steady as Philippe Petit across the world trade towers. Duane jumped out of the truck and again swung the back door open.

"I'm out of breath with excitement," she said. "If we are better than Bonnie and Clyde, we could pull off another caper at the same time."

"What are you talking about?"

"Another copy of that genetic machinery has shown up, like the two you just unloaded in Chicago."

He smiled, but then shook his head. "Nice espionage, however you determined that fact. But let's keep our sights straight. You don't want a dozen cops in here no more than I do."

Her chest heaved with displeasure. "All right. Like we planned, I'm grabbing one more box. I believe it is still safe to do so."

"I'll be waiting."

CHAPTER 12

Hook, Alex, and Cynthia padded across the rubber mat of the automatic doors. Approached by people coming into the hospital, they stepped aside for a young man pushing his father in a wheelchair, two energetic children running around their mother's legs, and a solo hospital worker wearing maintenance clothes. He wondered if it was the same man who had pointed out the dolly inside to them.

The man brushed by so close, Hook's sense of smell caught him off guard. Maybe it was the mother passing him that smelled faintly of lavender, and not the lean fellow with the baseball cap whose gaze followed the parallel lines of the rubber mat out the door.

Cynthia stayed behind Alex, but Hook had slowed, and she kept from bumping into her boyfriend. She always prided herself in her situational awareness, which was part of her being a fine laboratory scientist, and she made note of the cascade of visitors passing to the left. The three of them filtered out into the cloudless day, a gentle breeze stirring the trees dotting the parking lot.

"Until recently," Cynthia said, "my younger sister's the only one I used to see who toed in her foot that much."

"I believe that is the delivery truck." Hook pointed to the end of the circular drive of the hospital entrance. He turned to Cynthia. "What did you just say?"

"My sister is ridiculously pigeon-toed. Lately, I'm seeing people walking around here the same way."

"That is so unfair to pigeons," Alex said, "I have watched them many times without noticing that they are pigeon-toed."

Hook stepped ahead, rapped on the driver's side of the small truck, and then turned back to Alex. "In my noteworthy observational determination, I think you are correct. I think those birds walk with their toes pointing straight ahead."

"Whatever." Cynthia shook her head. "My sister's problem was so bad, she used to trip over herself!"

The driver grabbed a clipboard from the passenger's seat and slid out.

"I am Dr. Hookie. You are a sight for sore eyes if you are indeed the guardian angel delivering my NGS machine."

"Thank you. I have been called a lot of things, especially by my wife, but never 'a sight for sore eyes.'" He moved towards the sliding side door. "Because of the problem Dr. Hookie is having, I need to see your identification."

Hook didn't mind at all. "Excellent. I will be glad to."

"He is who he says he is," Cynthia chimed in. "The one and only infamous."

"Nevertheless…"

Hook pulled out his wallet and flashed his campus identification. The man smiled, swung the door open, and put his hand on the closest box. "You can borrow the dolly from the truck to wheel it inside."

"Your offer is much appreciated," Hook said.

Alex helped place the machine down. "I'll wait here," the man said, handing Hook the paperwork and a pen.

Hook scribbled his John Hancock, and gave them a thumbs up. "Success! I'm not letting this NHS machine out of my sight."

"Whatever makes you happy." The man smiled. "You are obviously devoted to your line of work, sir."

Alex began pushing the dolly. Single-file, they veered into the hospital and scooted through the hallway.

"I can carry this upstairs," Alex said, as Cynthia pushed the elevator button.

The three of them scanned the lobby where Bruce was driving a nail into the wall for a painting. The other worker was opening up a registration table for people passing through the doctor's office building. Alex grabbed the heavy box once the elevator landed on ground.

Hook wheeled the dolly around. "Thanks. I'll see you upstairs after I take this back to the delivery man."

Belinda passed Hook, Alex, and Cynthia at the hospital entrance and then inside, veered to the left, wanting nothing to do with the registration desk where Kent Wadsworth and his helper signed up passersby for Friday. Only one more pickup for art and her day would be done—as far as heists go.

Against the wall, she skipped the first oversized carton, and went to two boxes leaning against each other. She slipped her box cutter through the adhesive tape of one of them, and liked what she saw. Probably a set, she thought. She grabbed the two of them, and although bulky and difficult to manage, she was determined to get them out to Duane. Passing the tall lobby sculpture, she separated them and carried one in each hand. Her foot was about to touch the automatic door mat.

"Looks like you are having some difficulty," said a voice behind her. "I am going out as well—stick those on here."

Slightly, she turned her head. A dolly was at her heels and, ironically enough, Dr. Hookie was offering to help her with her pillaging. Not only was his equipment useful, but the old man was too.

She wasn't a practiced imitator of a man's voice, so she thought quickly again as to the best way not to speak too much. First, it was easier to put the paintings on the dolly. She laid them down, grumbled in a fake masculine voice "thanks," and stayed ahead of him.

"I'm delivering this to the truck over there," Hook said, and stalled for the man to take his two cartons off by the curb.

Belinda tipped her hand towards her cap, and took the two boxes, one in each hand.

"We are all being helpful today," Hook mentioned to the delivery driver leaning against his truck. "But I feel bad we made fun of that guy's gait a little while ago."

"What he doesn't know, won't hurt him, Dr. Hookie."

"So true."

The man heisted the dolly into his truck, Hook left, and Belinda hurried as best she could until Duane popped out of the truck and took the boxes straight out of her grip. Without a word, he stuck them into the van.

"I need a cup of coffee," he said.

"Duane! No way are we going back in there."

"You got your way and risked everything by going in for more stuff."

"And it worked, right?"

"Point taken. Which is why it will work for me to get a blazing cup of coffee."

"Damn it, Duane." She huffed out a big breath. "Then get me one too." She circled the van and planted herself in the passenger seat.

The strong aroma of disinfectant permeated Duane's nostrils, and the floor shined compared to earlier in the day as he sidestepped a new red warning cone opposite the window side of the hallway. A backlog of people slowed his progress because they had started to single file between the two buildings to avoid stepping on the wet areas.

He went to turn into the coffee shop, and gasped at seeing Bruce, who was walking the other way. If the hospital worker kept going to the hospital lobby, he might notice some art boxes missing, and he and Belinda would be better off being away from the hospital property by then.

Bruce's interest was glued on his cell phone, enough that people behind him grumbled for him to hurry up.

"Y'all are working hard for your employer," Duane interrupted him. "Veer in here for a coffee. My treat."

Bruce's eyes widened. No one ever went out of their way for him. "Don't mind if I take you up on that."

Duane stepped in behind two women in line, and Bruce took a spot behind him. The hospital worker needed to finish the message he was typing and kept racing his fingers across his keyboard.

For his and Belinda's order, Duane asked a second barista behind the counter for two Americanos with no room for milk. She cranked steaming water on top of the espresso shots and handed him the to-go cups. Thinking quickly about what to order for Bruce, his primary objective was to delay the man. "I'll pay for these now, and also the man behind me. Make him a venti cappuccino. Make it caramel vanilla."

He waved a bill in front of her. "Keep the change."

Bruce opened his mouth in surprise. "I'm not sure that's what I would have ordered, but thanks. I'll try it."

"You're welcome." Duane rushed out the door, a cup in each hand, like the Campus Bakery and Coffee Shop was on fire. He hoped the caramel vanilla cappuccino would take forever to make, but he figured it only bought him a little time. He also laughed at Bruce, who had no idea he'd been impersonated all morning by Belinda.

Out at the van, he opened the door and handed Belinda her coffee. "Wish you hadn't gone back in there," she scowled, "but this does look delicious."

He wiggled his cup into the cup holder, cranked on the engine, and looked over. "We need to get out of here fast."

Hook stepped away from the automatic doors with a sense of relief. Finally, his newest machine was safe and sound in the lab. Alex probably had unpacked it by now and had it ready to use. The number of people in the lobby had picked up, and it was reasonable to assume the hospital was going to put on a very successful health fair.

He could relax now, so he went straight over to Kent's table. He tightened the band on his ponytail and wore a smile as he peered at the two clipboards filling up with names and email addresses.

"Excellent," Hook said.

Kent pushed off from the chair, his soft leather shoes moving him to shake hands with the scientist. "I believe so too. And here's the plan." He slipped a drawing from the bottom pile of papers with a diagram of the lobby's set up.

"Your table will be in this front aisle or back aisle," he motioned, "depending on how you see it. One of our star attractions with an expensive giveaway."

Hook beamed. Besides the daily work he did, he loved exposing people to the marvels of genetic testing. Most people had no idea of the knowledge they could attain about their own bodies if they chose to be evaluated.

Behind them, moving into the lobby with a hot cup of flavorful venti cappuccino, Bruce took a sip of the hot beverage through the tiny hole in the cap. Although a bit too sweet for him, the drink was a break from his usual morning bland-black coffee. His colleague was staying in the other building to finish preparations, and he needed to start the measurements on the side wall of the main lobby. The placement of the nails to hang the new pictures must be perfect.

He set his cup on a table, and leaned down to his tool kit. Grabbing his hammer and a nail, he stood straight and scoured the wall. The first box against the wall held the painting that would be closest to the hallway. His eyes shot downward. He needed to lean the painting against the wall to estimate its placement.

A scowl crossed his face. The space was empty. He darted his eyes across the wall. For sure, only an old picture hung in the middle of the west end of the lobby, and that one, they'd instructed him, was going to come down.

He looked back to the floor, and down the line, and swerved around to scan behind him. A chill made goose bumps pop up on his forearms. Intermittent gaps were present in the line-up of the boxes. All of them were not there! "What the 'h?'" he mumbled.

Bruce took the lid off the coffee cup and slugged down a lick of the frothy topping. He placed it back down and walked the line, tipping the boxes there to check behind them. But he gulped, and scanned all around the large oval room.

Slipping off his baseball cap, he scratched his head, and headed over to Kent Wadsworth. If anyone knew what happened to the items while he was gone, it was the Associate Executive Director of Monument Medical Center.

At the fair's registration desk, Bruce paused as a visitor beat him to the table. Kent and Hook stopped talking.

"A health fair, huh?" said the elderly gentlemen. "Maybe I'll feel guilty about the donuts I eat every morning if I stop by."

Hook blinked. "Maybe you're not doing too badly."

"Easy for you to say. You're not walking around with an extra twenty pounds." The old man patted Hook as if he was thirty years younger than him and clasped the nearest pen. He scribbled his name on the form.

Bruce edged in between Hook and the man. "Mr. Wadsworth, did you ask someone to move a few of the paintings?"

Kent put his hand on his waist. "What are you talking about?"

Bruce flicked his finger toward the west wall as the old man next to him ambled away. Kent spun around to look. Wearing a question mark on his face, he turned back to his worker. "Seems like there may be empty spots over there but no one, that I am aware of, has moved a thing."

Kent widened his eyes with concern and Hook furrowed his brow and spoke.

"Are you talking about the bulky cardboard boxes that you just moved outside on the dolly I had borrowed?"

"What?!" Bruce blurted out.

"What's going on here?" Kent asked.

"I didn't move anything," Bruce said.

Kent turned to the woman helping him out. "You can handle it from here." He looked at Bruce. "Pull out your inventory sheet and let's go take a look. Come on Dr. Hookie. You too."

Bruce picked up his cappuccino. On the way across the room, he pulled out the list of items from his front pocket with his other hand. The three men huddled at the first empty space.

"We can't tell anything," Kent said, "until all these boxes are open. Then, by process of elimination, we'll be able to tell if anything is missing. Bruce, I can't ignore what Dr. Hookie said, either. I hope you are not pulling a fast one on the hospital."

"Mr. Wadsworth, I've been working here for four years. I can't believe you would think that."

"If we indeed have a problem," Hook said, "let's all calm down, and address the 'what' and the 'where' at the moment. If need be, we'll figure out the 'who' later."

However, Hook thought, he himself had helped the maintenance man move items out of the lobby. Out of his willingness to help people, had he enabled a crime?

Then, he wondered, there must be more men walking around helping with the health fair. But what were the odds that another one of them was wearing the same type clothes and baseball cap, and could double in size and stature?

Giving Bruce the benefit of the doubt, Hook realized he had not totally seen the man's face.

CHAPTER 13

Their search for boxes in the lobby and comparing what they found with Kent and Bruce's inventory sheet, told the group what they feared. Five pieces of artwork were missing.

Hook patted Kent's back. This time, the genetic scientist's equipment was free from larceny, but the Associate Executive Director of the hospital had suffered a blow. Businessmen in upper management of a big health care facility were immersed with accountability to a Board of Directors, and Dr. Hookie felt bad for the man.

"I'm sorry," Hook said. "Friday's fair has been your brainchild, and now there's a wrinkle in it. Let's call the police, and I will contact Sydney Monaco."

Kent stood paralyzed to the floor and gritted his teeth. Although in his late thirties, the few wrinkles on his face came to light, and he looked older. He raced his hand over his short-buzzed hair. "Of course. And where was Freddie Simpson? What is the point for the hospital to pay security guards who fail to secure our belongings?" He faced Hook and Bruce. "Those five pieces of artwork were no less than a thousand dollars a piece."

Both Hook and Bruce let him get it off his chest and remained silent.

Kent glanced down. "I'm not thinking straight. How about you, Dr. Hookie? Did your machinery arrive safely?"

"Yes, thank you. Now, call the police. I'll be in the coffee shop."

After buying a straight black coffee, Hook secured himself a corner table. He popped the lid off the cup and took a sip, and placed his call. Not only did he consider Sydney a friend, but he had the utmost faith in her skills. She could be silent as a lamb, but that didn't mean she was sleeping on the job.

Sydney answered promptly. "Dr. Hookie, what telepathy. Good morning."

"Morning to you too, Dr. Monaco, P.I. I bet that means you can furnish me with an update on your investigation. I, unfortunately, have worse news. New artwork slated to hang in the hospital lobby, in concert and in celebration with the health fair on Friday, was just stolen."

"Where are you?"

"Campus Coffee…"

"Take it slow on that coffee. I'm driving to the office, but I'll turn around and be there in ten minutes."

Hook hung up, put the lid back on the paper cup, and went to the counter and ordered a scone. The blueberry pastry kept him busy, and soon Sydney appeared. She wore brown, slim fit trousers, and a sporty suede jacket, and put down a flat, black leather bag on his table.

"You're late," he kidded her.

"Over my dead body."

Hook cracked a smile. "Have a seat. Can I buy you a coffee?"

"No. I'll be right back." She bought her own, and sat across from him.

"Kent is on the phone calling the police."

"We'll go talk to him. Did this happen in the lobby?"

"Yes. Cynthia and Alex were around too."

"Round them up. Let's go the scene of the crime and also look at the cameras." She dumped a sugar packet into her cup and stirred. "I am working on the previous robberies, Hook, but I also became slightly involved with the baby napping."

"I have faith in you, Sydney."

"The problem with the previous stolen campus equipment is that this thief, or these thieves, aren't huge criminals with a large network of medical technology to move or transport, so that they are not on most police or other investigative organization's radar."

"They may be small-time, yet they do heavy and disruptive damage to a facility like ours."

"Exactly. I'm still focusing on finding the stolen articles. Not only do I want the machinery back in the proper hands, but that would also lead us back to the crooks. I'm following leads through internet sites and contacting my sources in different cities. Etsy may be above board, but surprise sites are born every day for the turnover of stolen, expensive articles."

She rubbed her eyes. "A few nights ago, my eyes were dry as a desert after my hours spilled over past midnight. I tracked stolen items until my search winded up in a dead end."

"Sorry to hear that, but you're probably getting close. Cops are focusing on their investigation of the criminals, but I am disappointed in the slow progress."

Sydney's shoulders slouched down, and she lingered over her cup.

"Thievery aside," Hook said, "I always wonder how you continue to manage the disappearance of your parents. That must be so difficult, especially since you and your brother used your newfound investigative skills to look for them."

Hook knew, as well as Sydney, that her parent's cold case meant that someday their bodies could turn up, and the manner of their death may not be pretty. He shook his head, while Sydney avoided eye contact.

"Thank you for a bringing them up again. A day doesn't pass that I don't think about them. The work I do now is for them."

"They would be proud of you, just like I am."

"You're special, Hook. There aren't many older men around who keep plugging along and contributing to the scientific community like you do."

"Thanks." He smiled, and slid his phone in front of him. "Where do you want Alex and Cynthia to meet us?"

"The security room. Let's zoom in on new footage of the campus, particularly the lobby and exits."

He gave Alex a ring, and his assistant answered. "First off, is our new machine safe and sound?" Hook asked.

"Sure thing, Dr. Hookie. She's out of the box and is up and running."

"How about leaving the lab for a bit, and meeting Sydney and I in the room with the security cameras? Another robbery occurred down here after you both left."

"We'll be right there. Don't worry, I'll lock the lab."

Alex turned to Cynthia. "This should come as no surprise, but something downstairs was stolen after we left."

"Strange timing with the delivery of our machine. Good thing we brought it up here."

"I think that's what Hook was worried about. We need to meet him in the security room."

In the coffee shop, Hook and Sydney stood at the same time and headed to the lobby.

Kent and Bruce rushed in from the outside, where a police car was parked and the lights running across the top of the vehicle shut off.

"They want to talk to you all," Kent said, "but in the meantime, they're combing the area. Glad you could join us, Ms. Monaco. The items were stolen from boxes along the wall over there. This is dreadful, and it's causing a blemish on the hospital's reputation."

"Plus," Sydney mentioned, "it not only marks a change in the thief's M.O., but he, or she, or they, are becoming more brazen. Walk me through here, show me the other boxes, and tell me the hospital's plans for the rest of the week.

"You scientists stay here." Sydney darted her eyes to the floor, and they walked off. Hook, Cynthia, and Alex stood in a circle.

"Did she just put us in recess?" Alex grinned.

"She did." Cynthia frowned. "But I always learned that recess is for kids, and happy hour is for adults."

"Hold that thought," Alex quipped. "Let's go for Margaritas or Pina Colada's after work."

Cynthia bobbed her head. "Dr. Hookie, why don't you come with us?"

He shook his head. "I'll probably head home to the Mrs."

"But you could stop for just one drink. Don't live up to the reputation that scientists are all nerds looking over Petri dishes."

"I'm no nerd. My going out to party after work has more to do with my advancing age. I was doing really well until I turned seventy-years old and then my tail bone started to hurt."

Alex started to laugh. "That is actually amazing. I hope when I'm seventy, that's my only complaint. Plus, you're the sharpest guy I know over sixty."

"You're confusing being sharp or intelligent with something else. You see the gray or silver highlights in my ponytail?"

"Always."

"Those are wisdom highlights."

"Then you have it all, Dr. Hookie—wisdom, intelligence, and fine health—except for your tail bone."

Hook waved his hand at them, and smiled. "Where are you going after work?"

"I found a new Mexican restaurant down the road with a bar," Alex said.

"No promises, but I'm leaning that way."

"Leaning what way?" Sydney stepped into their conversation with Kent Wadsworth and Freddie on either side of her, but basically kept moving.

"For a drink after work," Hook said as he spun around. They formed a long train after her and invaded the security room.

The only man there swiveled in his chair. "My buddy left for an errand. Have a seat." He nodded at Hook and Sydney. "This group is showering me with attention these days."

"Unfortunately," Kent said, "we lost some artwork straight out of the lobby this morning. Not lost, but stolen."

"May I?" Sydney stole a chair in front of the screens.

Bruce squatted alongside her chair. "I was at work at seven-thirty, sorted through some boxes by eight o'clock, and then went over to the other side."

"That goes for me, too." Kent's eyes lighted up. "I started registering people for Friday's event right before eight o'clock."

"Where?"

"At the table which is set up as people walk in the front door."

Her fingers began working the monitors, and the man in the room observed and configured settings as well.

"We're starting at seven o'clock," Sydney said. "I didn't see cameras mounted on the walls in the general area. We can't observe back by the wall, can we?"

"No," the man told her. "We watch comings and goings at most entrances and exits."

She twisted her neck towards Kent. "Might think about more security cameras."

"That's the problem with health care these days. All the extras cost money, and those costs are incorporated into medical bills. Not only can people not afford it, but health insurance and Medicare can't afford it."

She frowned, looked forward, and studied the monitors. Health care workers, volunteers, elderly with assistance devices, and patients mostly came in, rather than went out, the front doors.

"Bruce, it looks like you're arriving right here." Sydney pointed to a tight group of three people coming in close together, and stopped the footage.

"No, that's not me."

Her head bobbed up to him and then back to the screen.

"I was here already. And I park in the back of the hospital. Came in the back way."

"What about the other guy you're working with?" Kent asked.

"He comes in the same entrance as me in the morning, but he's taller and stockier than me, and I don't think he's wearing a hat today."

Sydney started the camera again and the man started walking again through the entrance.

"Here we come," Hook said, "Cynthia, Alex, and myself. We passed this guy that resembles you, Bruce."

"The guy I joked about," Cynthia said, "who walks like my sister."

"We went out for the delivery of our NGS machine," Hook said.

"I see that," Sydney said in a few minutes as the threesome came under the camera's scrutiny again.

"We went upstairs with our delivery," Alex said, "and Hook was kind enough to bring the dolly back out to the driver."

"Did you see anything strange in the lobby as you passed?"

"Sorry, no. Nothing that we paid attention to."

"So here you come again, Dr. Hookie," Sydney said.

Everyone grimaced as they saw Hook being a Good Samaritan and offering the man an easier way to transport the boxes out the front door on the dolly he had used.

"Those are the boxes with the art work," Bruce said. "I'm sure of it."

"I could kick myself," Hook said.

"How could you have known any better?" Sydney asked. "This guy is a professional."

Hook glanced at Cynthia, his eyes narrowing. "Walks like your sister used to walk."

"What are you talking about?" Sydney asked.

"Birds. We stumbled on a conversation about pigeons."

Sydney allowed the footage to continue after Hook came back inside empty-handed of the dolly. When she started to get up, he looked her square in the eye.

"Mind if we go back to the video surveillance we checked out the other day when my NGS machine was stolen from the back delivery door—the 'baby at door' day?" Hook had it memorized in his head, but he needed to peel back the onion a bit more. Something now nagged at him, and he couldn't let it go.

Kent let out a disgruntled sigh and patted the counter. "We aren't getting anywhere, are we? This is going to be a nightmare to explain another theft to the board of directors. And if this leaks out, it may dampen the number of visitors who attend the health fair. And I'm sorry. All I'm getting out of our little meeting is that this criminal is a stealthy son-of-a-gun—virtually impossible to find."

Sydney and the security room man found the previous footage that they had earmarked from before. She let it roll and Hook watched closely, first the video from the parking lot and loading dock area, and then outside the ER when Freddie bumps into a woman standing outside. Wearing blue jeans and a yellow blouse, she places her hand on her head after he collides into her, and they exchange some words about the missing baby. The interlude finishes but Hook keeps watching as they go in different directions.

As the woman moves forward, his memory serves him well. He also remembers what Cynthia recently mentioned—about seeing pigeon-toed people lately walking around the campus.

Well, there was another one, he thought, as he studied the screen. The tall, curvy, yet slender blonde walking away from Freddie was toeing in with her right foot.

Virtually impossible? Hook wondered. Maybe he could figure out a way to hone in on this person after all.

CHAPTER 14

"I started a party," Alex said after work. He slapped a bill on the counter of the restaurant's bar. "I'm buying however many Margaritas this will pay for, and they are up for grabs."

After the bartender whisked up four of the tasty drinks, Alex, Cynthia, Bruce, and Kent grabbed one.

"I'll make up the slack." Hook placed another bill down. "Two more."

Sydney and Hook soon had their drink, and they all tapped their glasses together.

"I couldn't work with a better hospital group," Hook said, "and, of course, a better private investigator."

"How did you and Sydney meet?" Kent asked.

Hook set down his drink while the bartender placed two glasses of mixed nuts and cocktail napkins in front of them.

"Homeland Security consulted me on a case a few years ago, as well as Sydney. Of course, she was more valuable to them because she has both medical and criminal investigative skills, and little does she know it, but she reminds me of my daughter."

"I take it that's a good thing," Sydney said. "Hook impressed and scared me at the same time after we first met. We needed to meet with Homeland Security in D.C., and the fastest way to travel was by private plane. Hook arranged for one, and then flew us there himself. What a show off he was."

"What? You didn't like those light, trick maneuvers I did for your amusement?"

"Like I said. Show off."

"What did you do for Homeland Security?" Alex asked.

"It was before you worked in the lab. I did some genetic analysis for them, but up in D.C."

"Dr. Hookie is perfect for them," Sydney said, "because of his military experience as well."

"We've never flown with Dr. Hookie." Cynthia put on a mischievous smile. "How was his landing?"

"Ha! As rough as a rookie sailor on the high seas. I'll never board a plane again with him!"

Hook rolled his eyes, enjoyed another sip, and popped the nuts between his fingers into his mouth. "I better hurry home to Susan, Bentley, and my root beer soda."

"Who's Bentley?" Bruce asked.

"My tried and true cat. That feline waits for me at the door no different than a dog. When I step inside, he leads the way into the kitchen, which is my first stop."

"At which time Professor Hookie cooks dinner for his wife," Sydney said, "and probably the cat too."

"How did you know? I made grilled salmon the other night and I gave Bentley the first taste before I doused it in Thai sauce."

"We don't eat as upscale as your cat." Alex couldn't help but smile.

"That's because we're lousy cooks," Cynthia chimed in.

"Let's talk about Friday." Hook put down his glass and changed the subject. "How about I leave you in the lab, Alex? Cynthia can help me at our health fair table."

"That's fine," he told Hook.

"That'll be like a day off for me," Cynthia said.

Kent left his drink on a napkin, and placed his briefcase on the closest square table. He snapped it open, and extracted a file folder with papers. "I brought a comprehensive list of all the artwork purchased for the lobbies, and have circled the pieces that went missing today. Bruce and I made extra copies." He handed the file to Sydney.

"Perfect. Thank you."

"I'm out of here." Hook slid off the stool "It's been fun. I bet you are all going to stay and order nachos and burritos."

"We'll enjoy them for you." Cynthia watched their pony-tailed boss favor his right leg out the front door.

"I have my doubts about what we stole today," Duane said. "You better know what you're doing." He sat on Belinda's sofa, his legs spread wide, and nursed a beer he held in his hands. "There were two damn cop cars pulling in by the time I walked back out to the van from the coffee place."

"Which you shouldn't have gone back in to buy anyway," she snapped.

"Would you quit being so female?"

"What's that supposed to mean? That's part of your problem, you're always hitting on me *because* I am female."

"Hell, yeah. I'm talking about females always bossing guys around. You all think you own the planet."

"Shut up, Duane. If we were in charge, there'd be no World War One or World War Two in our history books, nor any other war."

"That's crap, Belinda. We'd have *more* wars, not less. Females are bitches and would start a war over who imports more tanning oil."

"This isn't going anywhere, so put a mug on your mouth." She stood on the opposite side of the table and began tapping her foot on the floor. That aggravated him as much as her words.

He finished the last few ounces and set the brown bottle down. "You got another beer?"

"Let's get the boxes out of the van first and unpack them. I need to take pictures and get them on internet sites."

He rose and, with heavy, deliberate steps, walked to her refrigerator and took out another beer, this time a can. His eyes stared at her as he popped the tab.

Belinda turned and went to the side door. She flung it open, stepped into the garage, and soon carried in one vertical-shaped box. "We're supposed to be a team. I'm the one who's going to be on the internet to midnight tonight getting all these details done, while you'll be finished for the day."

"Yeah? Well, who does all the drives to Chicago with the merchandise?"

"While I'm doing more brain work here figuring out our next hits, etc. etc."

"So take off tonight. Just take the pictures. And I think I should get away from you for a day or two. Maybe I need to get laid in Chicago."

"See? That's what's most important to you. Sometimes I wonder what your fifth grade report card looked like."

"Better than yours."

She frowned as she opened the first box, took out the painting, and snapped a picture. Perhaps he had a point. The rest of the week they should lie low. And why not send the artwork to Chicago anyway? Better than having it in her garage.

"How about driving our bounty over there? Leave in the morning? Let Linda and Dirk help out with the sale in addition to us?"

"Makes sense to me. No evidence in your garage in case we made any mistakes today."

"I'll put this back in the box, and you go grab another one from the van."

He did as he was told, happy with their plan. Belinda took a picture of each one. In the last carton, on the top lip of the frame, they found an inventory slip with the name of each of the pieces from the shipment. By process of elimination, she figured out the name and artists of the paintings they had in their possession and the price paid for each of them.

"Bingo!" she said. "This will really help." They kept only one end of each carton open as they slid the pictures back in. She taped up the ends when they finished.

Duane had long since finished his second beer and threw the can in the garbage. He stuck out his square chin and frowned. "I'll pack these in the van in the morning. Since I can't sleep here tonight, I'm leaving. I'll be over before the sun rises."

She nodded, relieved he was going without picking another fight.

"I'm stealing another beer for the road."

"Don't drink it while you're driving. All we need is for some cop to pull you over for drinking and driving."

He pulled out a beer and went straight out. "Now she tells me when I can't drink a beer," he mumbled as he closed the door behind him.

Belinda took off her shoes and padded over to her computer. She loaded the pictures, called her sister, and put it on speaker phone.

"Duane is headed over to you in the morning," she said. "What a great cache we obtained today—for the first time, all non-medical."

"It all went well?"

"As far as we can tell. I'm sending you the pictures right now." The email whooshed through with the colorful attachments. "I'm loading those on the internet art sites I've found, but do all you can in Chicago to sell them offline, separate from what I'm doing."

"Sure thing. If we don't need to ship them, that would be much better."

"And listen, go easy on Duane. He needs a vacation or a one-night stand."

"A one-night stand would be easier. Perhaps Dirk can arrange something. But, duh, all he needs to do is use one of those dating apps when he gets here. People getting on those are clear about what they are looking for. He can go home with a Chicago STD if he wants."

"That's hilarious, Linda. Just don't let him know we talked about this. He's angry enough at me."

Linda waited, poised over her computer. "No problem, and your email is here. Thanks. Those paintings look amazing. I should keep one for myself."

"You're not allowed to steal the stolen property."

"Night, sis. I'll start working on this before Duane shows up in Chicago with the merchandise.

Susan Hookie ambled across the room when she heard the garage door and Hook stepped into the house. "You're a bit late tonight, honey."

"Yes, dear." He landed a kiss on her cheek. "My crew met after work, mostly to discuss another theft at the medical campus."

"What is this world coming to? Even hospitals aren't safe."

She turned and walked in front of him, favoring each step. "My feet are tingling something awful today. I want to cut them off."

"Don't say such things. When did your doctor last check your hemoglobin a1c?"

"Don't worry about me or my lab values." She gave him a stare.

Bentley meowed at Hook from a wooden bench, waiting for an acknowledgment.

"You lazy thing," Hook said. "I'm supposed to greet you, huh?" He rubbed the top of the feline's head, and Bentley stood and arched his back with satisfaction.

Hook's cell phone rang from his back pocket, and he pulled it out.

"Sydney? Is the party over yet or is the group still feeding their faces?"

"The nacho bowl is empty, and we're all feasting on chicken and cheese burritos."

"So be it. You all needed to hear my voice again?"

Sydney chuckled. "No, we don't miss you that much. I thought you'd like to listen to some good news which the police department just told me. Kent here is ecstatically relieved. They found the hospital's amber alert infant who was taken the other day. The baby is safe and back in the pediatric unit for a thorough evaluation."

"That's wonderful news. Someone's in custody?"

"You bet. The baby girl was snatched by a young woman with a psychiatric history, and is unable to conceive."

"How'd they find her?"

"At least the woman had the good sense to bring the infant into a pediatrician, but he became suspicious and checked with the police."

"Perfect. That could not have worked out any better."

"Yes. We thought you would like to know."

Hook's eyes glued onto Susan. "Someone else is going to appreciate this news as well."

"Say hello to your wife, Hook."

"Will do." He ended the call, picked up Bentley, and cuddled him.

"What was that all about?" Susan asked.

"The stolen infant was recovered, and she's doing fine."

Susan's amber eyes glistened and she smiled. "I prayed for that baby." Her satisfaction was apparent to Hook as she bowed her head and nodded at the same time.

"Your prayers helped, I'm sure." Hook was not very religious, but he supported his wife's beliefs a hundred percent. He stepped into the kitchen and placed Bentley on the floor. "Let's conjure up dinner. If I make some pad Thai, will you help me cut up some greens?"

"Yes, bring it on," she said, "but let's make it without the noodles tonight."

"Okay, we'll make Jasmine rice."

They settled into a routine, but Hook carried the load.

CHAPTER 15

Linda Sisko's hair was swiped back in a barrette, and it held fast as she walked between the Chicago skyscrapers. A strong breeze blew between the buildings as she waited for the light to change at an intersection. She moved forward when the traffic stopped and headed across the street into her bank.

She was glad to see Rachel Foreman, the woman whom she had worked with last time. The blonde, curly-haired female had her eyes glued to a monitor, but looked up when Linda pulled out the chair across from her desk and sat down with a thump.

"Miss Foreman," she said, "how is your day in the banking business going so far?"

"Have a seat," Rachel replied, trying not to sound sarcastic. If there was one thing she had learned in the banking business, it was no different from other service industries where employees were not allowed to irritate the customer—who was always right, even when they were rude.

"My day job is going splendidly. Actually, I am a bit different from your typical 'banker' because I also deal with fraud investigations. Other than my day job, however, I'm immensely enjoying other aspects of my life. I'm remodeling the main area of my home. How about you?"

"Couldn't be better. I have another check to deposit into the new account you set up for me, but still haven't received the box of new checks and deposit slips in the mail."

"Another reason they call it snail mail."

"I suspect it is not the U.S. postal service's fault, but the slow pokes the bank hires to print their checks."

"Maybe so." Rachel forced a small smile. "Let me take that check for you." She filled in a generic deposit slip and, with the paperwork in hand, walked away to the back of the counter.

Linda glanced out the window to the pedestrians walking by in a hurry, and considered what the banker had mentioned about her redecorating project.

Rachel stopped alongside her and handed her the deposit ticket.

"Thank you," Linda said as Rachel slipped behind her desk. "By the way, I am not only in the medical equipment business. I have outstanding artwork to sell. Any of the pieces in my possession right now would make a stellar addition to your interior decorating project."

Rachel leaned back in her chair. "I am a fan of hanging things on my walls. Do you have a store where they are on display?"

"No, but the works will be gone in a flash once I display them on art auction sites."

Rachel had no desire to pursue that route, so she kept quiet. Plus, because of a crisis in her life a few years ago, she was more cautious and reserved around people than she used to be. She felt like ending the conversation with the woman who had poor manners when arriving at her desk.

"However, I can immediately show you photos," Linda added. She whipped out her cell phone and brought up Belinda's email with the pictures she'd sent.

Linda extended her arm and gave Rachel her phone. "Aren't they lovely? There are a variety of subjects and color schemes. And I offer them at wonderful prices that can't be beat."

Rachel flipped slowly through the pictures, her expression softening.

"There is a still life in there that would be perfect for you," Linda continued. "The pastel colors of the flower bouquet suits you to a T. The color scheme matches your blue-green eyes!"

Rachel was not keen on people giving her a pushy sales pitch, so she frowned. However, when she came to the vibrant colors of the flowers stretched across the picture Rachel was talking about, she hesitated. It was a still life that grabbed her attention and wouldn't let go.

She turned the phone to Rachel. "This one, right?"

"Yes. If I had the money right now, I'd buy it from myself."

Rachel wanted to roll her eyes, but she didn't. The woman was padding her bank account quite quickly, so she certainly had the money for a painting. "If I consider the purchase more keenly, how much is it?"

Linda calculated quickly. Everything stolen was income to the group, so she could 'discount' as much as she wanted. Most of the artworks' original invoice slips, per Belinda, were in the ball park of two to four-thousand dollars.

"That one is fifteen hundred dollars. A bargain from the original price of twenty-four hundred."

Rachel knew good artwork wasn't cheap, but since the picture was unplanned for in her budget, she flinched.

Linda quickly reconsidered. "I tell you what. I will give it away for one thousand dollars, but I can't go any lower than that."

Rachel could swing that price, and she really did like it. "I want to see it first."

"How about tomorrow? I'll bring it in."

"That suits me fine. I will be here."

Duane considered himself a master at spotting police vehicles on the highway, where they lurked at turnarounds in the middle of I-65 or alongside the road where vehicles joined into the flowing traffic. Crossing the Kentucky/Indiana state line, he had already covered seven hours of his drive to Chicago with the stolen artwork.

The middle part of the trip was the easiest, he thought, as he disengaged the van's cruise control and sped up. His own city of Atlanta, and Linda and Dirk's Chicago area, were the worst. Both cities always had roadwork going on, and were huge hassles to drive in and out of.

He floored the accelerator some more, passed the slower traffic on the right, and changed the radio station to country music. When he took his eyes off the screen and back to the front window, there he was. A cop car just waiting for him. Duane mumbled a four letter word and switched his foot to the brake to slow down.

After passing the marked police vehicle, it pulled out, and flicked on the colorful lights on top just for him. Duane kept going, but slowed, and carefully chose an even area next to the highway to pull over and stop.

While keeping his hands on the wheel, he monitored the rear view window as the cop sat and ran his plate. It seemed like forever, and each second which passed by also made his heart rate tick faster. His mind scrambled with anxiety. What should he say about his speed? What should he say if questioned about the boxes in his car? He needed to stay cool. Everything the group had been working on was in jeopardy and Belinda would kill him if she found out he'd been pulled over due to a reckless driving speed.

The car door opened and a police officer stepped out—a female police officer. Just his luck, he thought. The gender which was supposed to keep mankind out of wars would probably treat him with an iron fist in a velvet glove just like Belinda. He continued to stare and tried to contain his bounding pulse as she walked slowly up to his car door.

Duane rolled down the window.

"I've been waiting for you all day," she said.

Not only is she a woman, he thought, but she's a smart-ass cop, too. He could play that game as well as her. "I got here as fast as I could."

A tiny snicker passed over her lips. "How fast do you think you were going?"

"I thought I was going with the flow of traffic except to pass."

"I bet you know the routine. Driver's license and insurance card please."

"It's in my wallet, in my back pocket." His eyes flickered to outside, so she took a step back and let him slide out. She read the information he handed her while he scanned her up and down. The woman in blue had more muscle than he did.

"Why don't you wait back inside." Her eyes roamed to the back of the passenger van as he did as he was told. "So do you have anything illegal in the vehicle?"

Duane gulped, but made sure his facial expression didn't budge. "No, ma'am."

His heart pounded against his chest and, to his temporary relief, she walked back to her vehicle holding his information. It seemed like an eternity she was gone. It suited him fine as he tried to drum up a false story about the boxes in case she asked about them.

She came back to the van with a more relaxed stride and handed him his two cards. In addition, however, there was a speeding ticket. Duane almost blurted out an expletive, but held his tongue at the last second.

"So no drugs in the car?" she asked.

"Not now and never."

Believing him, she nodded. Her eyes narrowed as she looked at the boxes.

Duane worried in a hurry. He decided to offer information rather than have her think he was hiding something. "My girl and I are getting married soon, and are buying our own place. Bought some wall hangings for our house." He motioned his head in the direction of the boxes in the back.

"You could have bought more if you had decided not to speed today."

"Yes, ma'am."

She tapped the windowsill and walked away. Duane took a deep breath and rushed the air out with relief. He pulled back out onto the highway and programmed the posted speed limit into his cruise control.

One thing was for sure. Belinda was the last person in the world he would tell that he was served a speeding ticket while hauling their bounty to Chicago.

Duane made a second food stop in the late afternoon and couldn't bear to eat more food while driving. He sat at a McD's table and chomped down on a quarter pounder with cheese and a red container of twice-fried French fries. At least he had the two-out-of-four worst states in the country for declining human longevity behind him—Kentucky and Indiana. He used that data to excuse himself for what he was eating in the State of Illinois.

He popped back up to the counter and ordered a cup of coffee, which would be almost finished by the time he got back on the road. The entrance door opened and an Illinois state trooper entered, his waist burdened with a firearm. Looking to the left, the clean-cut officer walked to the table before Duane's and stopped. He struck up a conversation with a middle-aged couple, but Duane couldn't hear a word. The customer, he noticed, wore a tattoo on his neck like himself.

Duane shuddered at the officer being in the same location as him, and wondered what to do. Was his presence a coincidence or something more specific to do with him? He wrapped his hand around the yellow cup, secured the black cap, and slunk out the door.

In the van, he started the ignition and took off. "Damn," he cried, glancing back. "I can't even get to eat in peace." It annoyed him to no end as he continued his journey and figured Belinda had chomped down, undisturbed, on chicken teriyaki from her favorite Japanese take-out place. But at least no cop car had showed up behind him.

Half past eight p.m., Duane dragged his weary body and dirty van into Linda's driveway. He stretched out like a sore cat as he rang her front bell and glanced at the nice wooden chair on the porch. Maybe someday he would be as rich or set-up like the twins. But right now, he felt used and abused, and like the low man on the totem pole.

The door cracked open, and Linda waved him in. Her hand went to her waist. "I worried you wouldn't be here by tonight."

He took a double take. Sometimes he wondered which size-six sister was more desirable to him. If it were not for what Belinda had been through, it would probably be her. He was attracted to Linda, but never hit on her. The geographic distance between them would hinder any kind of relationship, plus he was never sure what the status was between her and Dirk Crouch.

"Dirk has waited on you. He's in the kitchen and can help unload the van."

They walked in where Dirk was trying to fix Linda's ice maker in the freezer. "Hey, buddy, how was the drive?"

Duane made a long face. "No fun. I'm wiped out, and the drive included two close calls with cops. Now I need to either appear in court to contest a speeding ticket, or pay the fine."

Linda's jaw dropped. "You idiot. Getting here didn't mean exposing us to potentially getting caught. You're paying the ticket, not going to court."

His eyes wandered downward and he sighed.

"I'm sorry, Duane. You're doing your best. I'll reimburse you for the ticket."

"Thanks, and do you have anything I can eat? I had to ditch my dinner because a cop showed up."

"Let's unload the goods," Dirk said, "get a beer and a meal, and then you can stay at my house overnight."

"All right." Duane followed Dirk out to the driveway. He liked his colleagues in Chicago a lot more than Belinda in Atlanta.

The next morning, Linda slid each picture up from its box, enough to see each one. The only one she cared about was the still life which she had half sold to the banker. Pottery pieces, which dotted her kitchen shelves and counters, were the only works of art that she had an inkling for, so when she found the piece in question, she slipped it right back down.

She finished dressing in tight leotard-type pants, and a soft overhead sweater. After booking a drive on her phone app with a ride-hailing company, she waited at the front door with the box beside her. No way would she drive downtown with the merchandise and then haul the package to the bank a few blocks away from a public parking lot.

A CRV showed up and the driver put her package in the back. "How you doing today, ma'am?" he asked when they piled into the car.

"Not too bad. How about yourself?"

"Need to make a few bucks this morning, so I'm here."

His jet black eyes settled on the rear view mirror. "I bet you'll be making more than a few."

"For only one hour of work on my part, you make a valid point."

"I need to work two jobs to make ends meet."

"Life isn't fair, is it? Either you need to inherit or win a ton of money, or you need to siphon it out of people in those two categories."

"I never thought of it in those terms. Which of the three do you fall into?"

"The third," she said without hesitation.

They drove in silence, the radio's music on low, and soon they were in the late morning downtown Chicago traffic. He pulled into a spot on the same street as the bank, and handed her the box from the back. "Feel free to use my services again," he said and laughed. "And especially if you need a colleague in whatever business you're in."

"I'll keep that in mind." She held her package and walked down the street as the vehicle pulled away.

In the front of the bank, she peered in through the glass window. Rachel Foreman stood beside her desk, rummaging through a pile of papers. Here goes nothing, she thought, and went in.

Linda appeared with a smile and teetered the box on the customer's chair in front of Rachel's desk. "Miss Foreman, good morning."

"Likewise, Miss Sisko."

"Since yesterday, you still have the first right to purchase this beauty in my box."

Rachel raised her eyebrows. The night before, she had imagined the painting on the empty wall above her fireplace where it would catch attention, and she was overdue to gift herself something nice that she really wanted.

Linda put the box on the floor and slid out the painting. She held it up and stepped back a few feet from Rachel.

Rachel immediately liked the colors, the subject matter, and the artist's painting style. "One thing we didn't discuss yesterday was the artist. Let me look the name up on the web to see what shows up."

"No problem."

Rachel read the name at the bottom right, slipped behind her desk, and googled the name. Several articles and sites came up, and she immediately clicked on the artist's website. He seemed to have made at least a small name for himself, and the prices of his paintings were as Linda had discussed.

"I'll write you a check," Rachel said. "I'll take it." She pulled out her checkbook from her purse in a bottom drawer, and after her signature, she handed it over. "No receipt?"

"I forgot my pad to write one up for you. You probably don't need one since your check will suffice as your record, and I bet you won't be returning it."

Rachel nodded because, most definitely, she was keeping it.

"Are we good?" Linda asked, as she slithered the canvas back in the box.

"Sure, and I suppose I'll see you soon with deposit checks from 'Necessary for Healthcare,' and other checks for separate medical equipment sales."

Linda parted with a nod and a handshake and waited for a ride home outside the bank. She whipped out her cell phone and called her sister. "Belinda, Duane delivered last night and I already sold a piece just now. I can't believe how easy that was."

"Awesome, sis. For how much?"

"A thousand dollars."

"Okay. That's not too bad. Congratulations to all of us—after all, it's team work."

"And do me a favor. Duane got a speeding ticket during his drive. I promised him we would reimburse him for it. So pay him when he returns to Atlanta."

"You are too kind. That kind of driving is going to get us in trouble."

"Lay off him. He's doing his best."

"You won't say that from behind bars."

"Whatever. Gotta go, my ride just pulled up."

Inside, Rachel Foreman leaned her new piece alongside her desk, happy as a kid with a new bicycle.

CHAPTER 16

Although Rachel pulled her new decoration out of the box that night, there were no picture hanging hooks in the laundry room drawer where she kept such things. It was not until the next day that she stopped at a hardware store, and brought home the supplies she needed.

She nursed a celebratory glass of wine for the beautification project of her home and, standing on a stepping stool, positioned the hook just right above the fireplace. Holding the canvas of pastel colors in her arms, she hung the picture, climbed down, and stepped back.

Enthusiastically, she smiled with pleasure. She had no regrets about the purchase. After putting the rest of the hardware package away, she picked up the painting's carton, and tried to collapse it into a smaller bundle for the trash in the garage. She ripped open the opposite closed end and, folded at the bottom, was a packing slip:

Monument Medical Center
c/o Kent Wadsworth, Associate Executive Director
3100 Summit Boulevard
Atlanta, GA 30115

In a flash, the slip piqued her investigative instincts. She tried to rationalize why it was in there—sometimes true explanations existed for what seemed like fishy circumstances. But maybe she'd been conned into buying something that did not belong to the seller.

Since it was after normal working hours, she folded the sheet and stuck it into her purse for the next day—at which time, she could either call the medical center in Atlanta and ask for Mr. Wadsworth, or call her friend Sydney Monaco, a private investigator in the same city. However, she may even call both of them.

Sydney Monaco walked into Kent Wadsworth's office on Thursday morning juggling a cardboard cup holder with two hot coffees in one hand,

and her briefcase in the other. "From your campus coffee shop downstairs. My treat."

"I should be buying for you. I also gave Dr. Hookie a call to come join us, and he's on his way."

"Since he's coming from the doctor's office building, I bet he'll stop and buy his own."

Kent sprung up from his chair and cleared papers off the other chair as Hook ambled in. He carried a gray cup holder as well and set it on the desk. "Three dark roasts. Nothing fancy."

The Associate Director pursed his lips and grumbled. "Y'all are trying to make me feel bad. If I knew we were doing a coffee gift exchange, I would have reciprocated."

"Next time," Hook said, sitting down. "Tomorrow's the big day."

"We've advertised the heck out of it," Kent added, "and the health fair is slotted to be our best one yet."

"All the more reason to make sure things go smoothly," Sydney said. "As both a physician and as an investigator, I am wholeheartedly interested in your fair being successful and without any merchandise suddenly going missing. I believe if the perpetrator we're after is going to make a hit, they may do it in one of the departments away from the festivities on the first floors. Your two security guards, the police officer who will be here, and I, have discussed this and will be making rounds appropriately."

Kent popped off the lid on his cup, sipped, and addressed Hook. "Are you okay with leaving your lab unattended tomorrow?"

"Alex will stay there, and Cynthia will be downstairs with me. Tomorrow, I'm not worried about our equipment."

The landline phone on Kent's desk rang, and he ignored the ringing. Beyond his office door outside, the area's receptionist answered his call.

"Mr. Wadsworth's office," the perky young woman said.

"Hello," the voice on the other end said. "Is Mr. Kent Wadsworth there?"

"He's in a meeting. May I ask who's calling?"

"My name is Rachel Foreman. I live in Chicago and would like to ask him a question about a painting."

"I don't think he's taking calls, but let me double-check." She put the call on hold, knocked on Kent's door, and stuck her head in. "Sorry to disturb you, Mr. Wadsworth. Some woman from Chicago would like to talk to you."

"Not now, Jenna. Just jot down her name and number. As a matter of fact, unless it's an emergency, or the President, or a Board member, I'll return calls next week after this fair is behind us. All my eggs are in one basket for now. And help yourself to one of these extra coffees we have." He pointed to his desk.

"Thank you." She left with a black coffee, and picked up the handset again. "Ms. Foreman, he can't take calls, but promises to return your call next week."

"Okay," Rachel said with disappointment.

"What's your number?" Jenna inquired.

When they hung up, the receptionist began a phone message pile for Kent to take care of the following week.

Belinda had better things to do than to keep tabs on Duane, or to drive over to his apartment to light a fire under his dumb behind. She parked in the skimpy lot and, although he lived on the first floor of the complex, she tried to remember which unit was his. A breezeway made up the spaces between each double unit, and scrubby bushes wound their way around the lodgings. The most presentable part of the real estate was the colorful sign out front which was freshly painted and had a new wooden border.

Seeing number "8" on the door, along with a three-inch vertical sign hanging down by a piece of twine, she knocked with a heavy rap. She shook her head as she waited and read "Enter at Your Own Risk" several times.

The door swung open, and Duane stood there and widened his eyes.

"You haven't answered my phone calls today," Belinda said, her hand on her waist. "You sick or something?"

"Nooo. How about I needed to nap after all the driving I've done this week?"

She walked into the dim-lit room where a take-out food container sat open on a coffee table. The plastic spoon was in his hand. "Speaking of your driving, I heard you got a speeding ticket. You want to land us all in jail or something? If that's what you want, don't take the rest of us with you."

Duane scowled. It wasn't Linda's fault, but he wished she hadn't mentioned that to the piranha in front of him who was growing sharper teeth by the day. He ignored her and went back to his food.

"My sister is so nice, she wants me to pay you for the ticket."

"You should take lessons from her."

"And perhaps you should be more like Dirk, who doesn't cause any trouble."

"All right already."

She eyed the gooey sweet and sour pork in the container. "Let's call a truce and not argue, and tomorrow, let's not get into any undesirable predicaments. I'm going to the health fair on the medical campus to get whatever free stuff they are doling out. I assume you are going, so scout around for ideas of what we could easily steal in the future."

He speared a lump with his fork and stuck it in his mouth with a bit of rice.

"By the way, that looks awful."

Duane shrugged. "Want some?"

From a marketing and advertising point of view, Friday morning rolled around with the most gracious start to the day—all sunshine and no clouds. And the temperature, Hook guessed, was around fifty-five degrees.

He bypassed the coffee shop and rode straight up to the lab where Alex was donning his white short jacket for the day. Cynthia stared into the small mirror on the wall and was adjusting her pink-streaked hairpiece hanging along the side of her face.

"Thanks for showing up early," Hook said. "Sorry to leave you with a stack of analyses today, Alex."

"It will be like a morgue in here today, but maybe I'll get more done."

"Without your main distraction?" He nodded toward Cynthia and smiled. "Probably so."

Hook grabbed his white coat from his office and a duffel bag already packed, full of materials for their table. Cynthia picked up two signs and the stands they would sit on, and they waved good-bye to Alex. "Come visit us at lunchtime," she said.

"Eight to four will be a tedious day," Cynthia said as they boarded the elevator. "I am used to the hours flying along in a lab, but dealing with the public is not my thing."

"The time will fly by, you'll see. You aren't as nerdy as you think."

The elevator doors opened up, and they fell behind medical personnel going in the same direction.

"Shall we grab coffee now," Cynthia motioned, "or shall I go back for it once we're set up?"

Hook made a hard left into the Campus Coffee and Bakery Shop and stood in line.

"I guess that answers my question."

"Actually, I don't want us to be apart or out of close contact today, so we'll pick up our first energy formula together right now."

Cynthia scrunched her eyes together. "But now I have two questions. Why must I be attached to your white coat today, and how are we going to carry our cups?"

The second barista was free and asked them for their order.

"How about a tall Americano," he said.

"Make that a double today," Cynthia said.

After putting down the supply bag, Hook grabbed a bill and put it on the counter. "Would you mind bringing them to our table in the lobby with two scones?"

She eyed the bill and nodded. "Sure, Dr. Hookie."

Hook and Cynthia proceeded to the hospital lobby where last minute details from health care workers, business departments, and vendors were taking place. White or solid color tablecloths donned the tables, and equipment, signs, and free items were everywhere. Papers stacked on clipboards asked for customers contact information, and baskets dotted tables for raffle ticket stubs. Bowls contained free pens, refrigerator magnets, and miniature candy bars like Halloween was imminent.

The table representing their laboratory had a crisp white tablecloth on it just like Dr. Hookie had requested, but he wondered about sitting most of the day on an aluminum chair. He would need to alternate sitting and standing, he figured, because his "disabled" leg always needed the variety.

With the two signs on opposite ends of the table, and the other items unpacked, Hook and Cynthia eyed the table from the front, pleased with it all.

"Here you go," the barista said. She placed down their items and wiped her hands on her apron. "If you don't have our number, Dr. Hookie, here's our card. Call us today if we can break away to bring you something."

"Much appreciated."

She walked off, and Hook took a moment to scan the walls. The artwork, the ones not stolen, hung nicely throughout the lobby and Kent Wadsworth had done well with the selection. Nearest to their table, was a painting of a mother and two children holding her hands. They stood on a beach with gentle waves rolling in towards their bare feet, their backs to the viewer.

Hook pointed at the wall. "Lovely, isn't it?" he asked Cynthia.

"Yes. Someday that may be me. I want two children, Dr. Hookie."

"I take it, Alex will be the lucky dad."

She smiled, her eyes twinkling in anticipation of her future wants and desires.

"Live every minute like you mean it," he said. "Before you know it, you'll be an old person like me."

She took a bite of the fresh scone in front of her while Hook placed an empty glass bowl in the forefront and a roll of red tickets next to it, which were for his free genetic analysis raffle. Kent Wadsworth was at his table up near the entrance, and waved back to them.

"Dr. Hookie, why must we be a close team today like you mentioned?"

Hook made direct eye contact with her. "Recently, you made comments about people walking around here who are pigeon-toed."

"Yes, even when we watched the security videos." She tilted her head, waiting.

"Can you keep a keen eye out today for anyone who fits that toed-in description and tell me immediately? I will be watching how people walk as well."

She paused putting the next bite in her mouth. "Phew, what an easy request."

Hook opened the lid on his coffee and eased into the chair. She held back asking him any more questions because the subject seemed to be closed.

On Friday, Belinda woke in an excellent mood, dressed, and called Duane. "What the heck, do you want to ride with me? I'll pick you up."

"Since we don't need the van, sure. You didn't suffer a stroke overnight, did you?"

"No. I dreamed you were drowning in a washing machine, and I plucked you out and threw you in the dryer."

"How thoughtful of you. I'll be waiting outside." He failed to see why she was so psyched up about a health fair, and thought that less time on the campus would be a better alternative for her.

She soon pulled into his lot, and they headed southwest. "What time did this thing start?" Duane asked.

"Eight o'clock. We'll be there by ten at which time we can separate. However, I do want to walk around with a coffee."

"Me too. You drove, and paid for my speeding ticket, so I'm buying. Then you can pretend you don't know me or something."

Belinda decided to *try* to live by their truce today, and didn't argue. After parking, they walked to the closest entrance—the doctor's office building—and entered the lobby. He stayed behind her as she glanced at the tables, which seemed mostly informational for the doctors' sub specialty practices in the building. The surgeon groups were prominent, especially for orthopedics and sports medicine, and customers saw first-hand how plastic bone models demonstrated the benefit of "new" joints.

Inside the coffee shop, almost all the seats were taken. The rich smell of coffee filled the air, and Belinda and Duane stepped to the counter.

"A double shot espresso," the barista said to Duane.

"How'd you know?" he asked.

"I remember that order goes with that tattoo."

"Darn smart of you." He patted the ship's anchor on his neck like it was a trophy.

"And your lady?"

Great, Belinda thought, now we're a couple. "I'll take a tall mocha cappuccino."

He paid and left her a handsome tip in the jar. The barista's morning for tips was proceeding along very nicely.

Belinda pulled ahead of him and traipsed straight to the entrance where she wanted to start at the beginning. She made the table manned by Kent Wadsworth her first stop.

CHAPTER 17

Belinda hovered behind a woman and a toddler in a stroller. The young mother studied a hospital pamphlet on their pediatric services.

Kent encouraged Belinda with a smile. "Feel free to step up. Learn more about the area's best available health care. After all, our ER is open 24/7 and is the portal to emergency care."

Belinda smiled and checked out his name tag. "Mr. Wadsworth, I am already a fan of your facility."

"Really? What makes you appreciate us?"

She twisted her mouth at her stupidity to say such a thing, and elected to deviate an answer to the facility's appearance. "I passed through here a week ago, and now marvel at the new interior decorating job you've done here in the lobby."

"Staff put the paintings up in the last two days. Where do you go for your medical care?"

"I'm taken care of, but I'll consider Monument Medical Center for my future needs. Do I still qualify to throw my name in a pot for this free Bed and Breakfast weekend you're raffling off?" She leaned over and began writing out a ticket, and decided to use the name "Becky." That was the name she had used with the campus security guard outside the ER on one of their NGS heists. She filled in her cell phone number, which she figured did not pose a problem.

"Yes, be my guest to the hospital drawing, and make your way around. Best to start down this front aisle. Next stop, medical staff will take your blood pressure, your heart rate, and oxygen saturation."

She clasped her coffee, took a sip, and walked around the stroller. At the next table, she sat down and extended her arm. "Nothing like a free little check up."

A middle-aged woman with braided hair wrapped a cuff around her arm and soon announced "one-eighteen over eighty-two. Wish we all had numbers like that."

"I'm lucky to have a blood pressure at all." With other good numbers, Belinda reached for a free notepad and pen, and dropped them into her bag. The clutter in the front aisle ramped up and, not wanting her coffee to be bumped from her hand, she strolled to the life-size sculpture to chug down the residual coffee.

Sydney Monaco lingered at the hospital entrance, intermittently walking the curb outside, or the front area of the lobby. She spoke up when Belinda walked over. "The sculpture captures the loving bond between a mother and her child, doesn't it?"

"Yes, it does, as well as that new painting over there on the wall—the seashore one."

Sydney's investigative skills could cut to the chase immediately. "You must be a regular worker or patient here to realize that the hospital staff just hung that new painting."

"No, someone just mentioned that fact to me. Are you enjoying the fair?"

"Yes, but I have yet to visit every table. How about you?"

"I'm just starting." She hoisted her empty coffee cup as a good-bye and walked away quickly. She pitched the cup in the trash in the corner of the room.

Every few minutes when the activity at their table subsided, and after Hook encouraged her, Cynthia walked to either end of their back aisle to get a better view of the customers walking around the foyer. It was not as easy as she had thought, because women or men were often standing too stationary at a table.

Her eyes keenly focused when she spotted Sydney for the first time standing near the front door. A woman stood next to her, and they were exchanging words. The tall, pretty woman then parted her company and beelined towards the garbage can with her empty cup. Cynthia's eyes widened like a blossoming flower, and she hurried up front. She was sure the woman walked like the others she had seen recently on the campus— the ones who had reminded her of her younger sister's pigeon-toed style of walking. What was going on? She wondered. Was there an epidemic of people almost tripping over their right foot?

She forgot she had carried the last piece of scone she hadn't eaten. It gave her an excuse to stand still near the front window and nibble as the customer lady walked right by her. There was no doubt about the woman's gait, so she made her way back to Hook to tell him.

"I found you an intoer," she said, brushing crumbs off her hands.

"Excellent. Male or female?"

"Female."

"Does she point in her left or right foot?"

"Right foot."

"A common theme these days."

"I thought the same thing, and I took note because my sister is the opposite."

She scrutinized his expression. "But how would you know they've been right footed, when I thought I was the only one really noticing?"

"The security camera footage."

Cynthia wondered what Hook was thinking.

"Point her out discreetly," he asked.

"She's the only person at the table next to Kent Wadsworth."

"Smart woman. She's getting a blood sample drawn for a ridiculously cheap chemistry profile." Since she was sitting, Hook could not totally see her until she stood. When the tourniquet came off her arm, and the lab tech placed a wad of cotton and an elastic colored bandage, she rose. Hook ambled away and scrutinized her from a better vantage point.

He guessed her to be in her early thirties and her gait fit Cynthia's description. Her hair, soft and curly, was a reddish-brown and cut at her chin line. Studious-looking glasses framed her eyes, and she wore a subdued red lipstick. Although brown flats donned her feet, she was above an average woman's height, and wore dark trousers with a leather belt. Her cream-colored turtleneck fit her like a glove, and he noted the shape of her probable C-cup breast size, round and perfect like a baby's butt.

Belinda showed interest in a health care worker who asked her if she wanted to do a pulmonary function test for only ten dollars. She agreed, and Hook kept walking. He turned at the end of the aisle and went back to his own table.

Hook nodded at Cynthia as he slipped behind the tablecloth and a couple stopped before them. A middle-aged man had his hand on his wife's waist as they peered at Hook's materials.

"Please take a raffle ticket," Dr. Hookie said. "There will be a drawing at the end of the day for a free DNA analysis. Research has skyrocketed, and we can dole out important information regarding a person's risk for certain cancers. If you win, I will also sit down with you and take a thorough family history."

The man dropped his hand off his wife's hip and grabbed a pen. The woman tilted her head at Hook.

"In general, ma'am," he said, "a lifetime breast cancer risk is up to eighty-seven percent if you carry a specific high risk gene."

"That *is* a high statistic." She also pulled a ticket from the roll and let her husband fill out her information. "But then what is my risk if I don't have a problematic gene or a family history of breast cancer?"

"Smart question. A woman has a one-in-eight chance of developing breast cancer, but one in ten women diagnosed are under the age of forty-five." He contracted his brow, showing his displeasure.

"We hate that probability in the research business," Cynthia added.

"However," Hook continued, "our analysis can tip us off about other associated cancer risks—such as colorectal, pancreatic, and kidney cancer, and something people often forget to consider—male breast cancer."

The man dropped their tickets into the glass bowl and held onto their stubs. Beyond them, Hook laid eyes on Belinda, who had skipped several aisles, and was leaving the table next to him. He pulled in a deep breath. "Thank you," he told the couple. "Good luck with the raffle and enjoy the rest of the fair."

The man picked up a pamphlet about Hook's lab work, clasped his wife's hand, and they left. Dr. Hookie glanced down at the approaching feet of his next customer as she pulled up in front of them. It was now or never.

"Morning, ma'am," Hook said immediately. "You are extremely fortunate today because you are around the twelfth person to stop here at our table." He spoke with his best soft-spoken voice, the tone he used with his wife.

"We have a raffle going today, but that will be for only one person's name who will be pulled from our glass jar. However, I had decided beforehand to allow a second prize. It is for a free, thorough, and comprehensive genetic analysis—to be given to the twelfth person to show up here today. The testing costs thousands of dollars, and you have just won the honor. Congratulations!"

Cynthia's eyes wandered over to him as she wondered what her boss was doing.

At first, Belinda's neck craned forward to read Hook's poster, but by the time he said 'congratulations,' she was totally focused on the elderly scientist. She rarely won anything or had good luck. Maybe that was part of the reason she had developed the habit of taking what she wanted.

"I am not sure that I need genetic testing," she said.

"You may not *need* it, but you could use it. Scientia potential est."

She shrugged her shoulders. "And that means ...?"

"Knowledge is power. It's a Latin aphorism. In the future, you may regret not having it done, and here I offer it to you for free."

"I'm all for 'free,' but I suspect you only do your voodoo crystal ball to tell women if they possess an increased risk of coming down with breast cancer, right?"

"Breast cancer risk is only one small fraction of the overall picture. Particular gene results will tell us if you have an increased risk for melanoma, for instance. Malignant melanoma is still an awful skin cancer, and may or may not be related to how much sun exposure you have had in your lifetime. One of the factors which can increase *your* risk is staring at me right now—your fair skin."

Hook took the opportunity to study her face—a few freckles dotted the top of her cheeks, and she had a residual, faint birthmark off to the left side of her eye.

"I will test certain genes," he said, "to determine if they have any abnormalities, which are related to melanoma. Another terrible female cancer is ovarian. You don't want to get it, but you want to know if you're at risk."

She began to move her head in a slow, steady nod.

Cynthia took a sidestep. "Dr. Hookie is the go-to person in this field. Included in your analysis will be your percentage chances also, if a particular gene is defective, of pancreatic, colorectal, uterine, thyroid, leukemia, adrenocortical, brain, other GI cancers, and sarcoma." She rattled them off as expertly as Hook.

"I'm sold, and I should be thanking you for this opportunity. One more question, however. What if I test positive for something? How will that change anything?"

"If we find a mutation associated with an increased risk for a certain type of cancer, then we can implement cancer screening and prevention based on that specific test result, and we can recommend genetic counseling or consideration of genetic testing for family members. Do you have any children?"

"No," she said, followed by a chuckle.

"Any siblings?"

She twitched her shoulder, not wanting to divulge anymore personal information to the elderly geneticist in front of her—the very man in charge of the lab whose NGS machines she had stolen twice. Now Hook offered her a service which depended on that very high-tech piece of equipment she had plucked right out from under him. Belinda wanted to laugh but, instead, a small snicker passed her lips.

Hook waited for an answer to his question, but none came.

"I would be crazy not to take your free analysis," she said. "Too bad I have to be stuck again because I just gave blood for testing at another table."

"No problem! I will take a sample of your saliva."

"Spit? What'll they think of next?"

Cynthia grabbed a small box from the back of the table, pulled out a tube, and handed it to her boss.

"Please fill out this information," he said, placing a slip in front of her.

She used the available pen and wrote in her details. It asked for a name, address, and telephone number, but she only wrote her name and cell phone number and handed it to him.

Hook didn't mind the lack of an address, and didn't press her for it. "I want you to gather your saliva in the front of your mouth and spit it in here. The foam won't count. You must fill this tube to the line right here," he pointed.

She proved to be an excellent spitter and, with the deed done, Hook immediately capped it.

"Now what?" she asked.

"We will do the analysis, as well as the other person's analysis who wins our raffle. I will call your number when I'm finished, ask you to come into my office to discuss the results. This is a working phone number, correct?"

"Of course. It's my cell phone number. How long will it take?"

"Since this is part of our big prize, I will personally see to these analyses as soon as possible, which may mean results available on Monday."

Cynthia's eyes narrowed. Was her boss planning on working overtime?

"Way cool," Belinda said.

Hook eyed her information again. "Thank you for participating, Miss Sisko. May I call you Miss? You are not married, are you?"

"Ha, ha. Someone who works with me would like that from me, but there's no chance."

"Whatever floats your boat. Marriage is not for everyone. Enjoy the rest of our health fair."

"Bye," she said, and slipped the pen she held into her bag.

He watched her step away and appreciated her signature gait as she became lost in the growing crowd.

CHAPTER 18

After being diligent at the entrance all morning, Sydney Monaco decided to make rounds on the tables in the hospital lobby. She had sat on the lip of the low windowsill and had scarfed down a turkey sandwich and coffee, and now scooted over to Dr. Hookie's table.

"Your table has garnered a lot of attention all day," she said.

"Yes," Hook said. "Cynthia and I are happy about the buzz we generated about what we do. Have you seen anything suspicious?"

"Not a thing. No one has passed me with any materials that appear to be stolen. And Freddie is carefully monitoring the back entrance and reports no problems. And, a police officer is ambling about the entrance to the doctor's building and the hallways, and we are clear there as well."

"Thank you for your diligence. What would you say if I set us all up for a tentative meeting on Monday? The ETA to be determined over the weekend?"

"Makes sense. We can share notes about today, update any missing equipment details, and make a plan for going forward. I'll work extra over the weekend regarding the deep internet search I'm making for the stolen paintings and medical devices."

"Perfect. I'll put in a few extra hours as well."

"Dr. Hookie, is there something I can do?" Cynthia interjected. "Your weekend should be your own."

"Not always."

She rolled her eyes.

"Cynthia, most of my enjoyment, including an added weekend, comes from working with that double helix that Watson and Crick discovered only in the past one hundred years. My whole adult life, DNA winds up my thought process in its strands and won't let go. When I die, I want an etching of the helix wrapped around my name on my stone monument."

"Does your wife know that?" Sydney asked.

He laughed. "No. I better tell her!"

"Yes. But knowing you, you will probably outlive us all."

He shook his head, making his ponytail slip back and forth on his shoulders, as two young adults stopped behind Sydney.

"I better go," Sydney said. "I'll leave leeway in my schedule on Monday and await your call. Do you want me to tell the others? I'm going over to Kent's table."

"Yes. Absolutely. And talk with at least one police officer roaming around as well."

She narrowed her eyes. Hook Hookie really wanted a thorough meeting on Monday, and was leaving no one out.

The number of visitors on the first floors of Monument Medical Center dwindled down to a trickle of folks who were there for other reasons as the health care workers and vendors packed away the materials on their tables. Bruce folded the empty tables and began stacking them against the wall. The goal was to have everything back to normal within an hour of the health fair's closing time of 4 p.m.

The last thing Hook did before leaving the lobby with Cynthia was to have her draw a name for the winner of the raffle. He called and spoke to a woman who couldn't be happier that she had won something, and arranged for her to come in next week to give him a saliva sample.

Hook and Cynthia again split the items they needed to carry back up to the lab and sauntered over to the elevator. "That woman I just spoke with would have been happy if she'd even won a free bus ride to the campus. It doesn't take much to satisfy some people."

"And, hopefully, our analysis proves useful to her."

They rode the elevator up and Alex helped unpack their materials. Hook went into his office with Belinda's sample, and called his wife.

"Susan, I am going to stay here in the lab this evening and do some work which popped up."

"But didn't you have that health fair today? She asked. "Aren't you finished?"

"Yes, we are done—all the more reason I need to catch up here."

"You haven't worked late in a year or two, but I understand. I will surprise you and bring you something to eat."

"I won't famish. Don't worry about me."

"No. How about if I buy us hot brisket subs from that nearby chain sandwich place?"

"All right dear. If you think your diabetes can stand it. Don't forget, my lab is on the top floor of the doctor's office building."

"I think I'll remember it when I get there. I'll see you in an hour or two."

"Take your time." He hung up, brought the sample back out to the lab, and addressed Alex. "Did everything go fine up here today?"

"I got a lot done, Dr. Hookie. But Cynthia just said you are going to work late. Is there something I can help you with?"

"No, but thanks anyway. You two run along. Susan just told me she's going to surprise me with a submarine sandwich for dinner."

"Quite the surprise," Cynthia said.

Hook laughed. "My thoughts exactly. She means well and does her best. I don't think any of her surprises have ever been a surprise."

The couple headed to the door, and Hook hollered one more thing. "Sometime on Monday, we'll all meet for a joint discussion. A compilation of what's going on with the Monument Medical Center thief."

Alex waved his hand and they disappeared out the door.

Alone in his lab, Hook held the precious specimen in his hand and put it up to the light. He still marveled at the sheer awe of a spit sample and what it could divulge in these modern times. Watson and Crick would roll over in their graves if they knew what they started with the discovery of DNA. The science unfolding to do with the paired amino acids was mind boggling, he thought, and would again be more staggering by the time his old body wound up on the other side of the ground.

He planned out his time, also with the realization that Susan would be visiting him sometime soon. First, and foremost, he needed to isolate Belinda's DNA. Hovering over the lab counter, he used a primer to attach to the DNA with the purpose of eliminating the junk in the specimen. He lost track of time, and it seemed like minutes later when he heard his wife's voice.

"I did it. I found you."

Hook scurried over and took the paper bag out of her hand. The smell of barbecue filtered to his nostrils.

"Welcome back to my home away from home. It's been a long time, dear." He brushed his lips on her cheek, and ushered her in. "While my machine is running, we can go into my office and eat."

She glanced from side to side at the environment he worked in, and let her thin shoulder bag slip down off the untucked, checkered blouse she wore. Grasping the strap in her hand, she put it down on one of his chairs, and took a seat.

He cleared a segment of his desk and unpacked the bag. Two white containers held their sandwiches, and he put one in front of her. "I keep my little refrigerator stocked with drinks." He grabbed a root beer soda, and frowned. "However, I don't keep diet soda. I'm sorry about that. But here's a bottled water."

"Next best thing," she said.

"I'll be back in a moment. Please start without me." He rubbed his leg after getting up, and went back to his work area. Running the sample though the spectroscopy, he needed to find out exactly how much DNA he was dealing with. He went back to Susan, noting the dusky sky outside his wide windows, and again took a seat.

She had a half mouth full and, by the looks of it, seemed happy with her choice. Hook took a bite and raised his can of soda with approval.

Susan wiped her napkin across her lips. "Once you told me about a centrifuge machine. Are you using that tonight?"

"You remember correctly. Yes, that machine, tonight as always, gets used a lot."

"You explained it to me once—that it spins and spins and spins— whatever sample you put inside it."

"Yes. This is true."

"It is too bad I never went on with my education after the two years I spent at a community college."

"Life sometimes gets in the way, dear, which is not your fault." Their words about her education came up every few months, and Hook knew the subject was touchy for her. Susan had ended up caring for her mother, who had disabling Parkinson's disease, and it sidetracked the rest of her college education. "Your life at that time had a different purpose," he added.

She nodded, and took solace with his words. They finished their sandwiches and drinks with less talk, and Susan rose and peered at the pictures in his office. "Well, I better get home to Bentley. What time will I see you? Should I go to bed myself?"

"Yes, dear. That would be best, and don't worry about me. Thank you for dinner, and give Bentley a hug in the interim. I won't disturb you when I sneak in." He slid her bag up on her shoulder, and gave her a hug.

She hugged him back, and he walked her out the lab door. After the elevator doors closed, Hook went back to work. When he finished his first whole round of testing, a half-moon hung overhead in the night sky, and he made himself abort any more studying of Belinda's saliva. He'd be back over the weekend.

Saturday, Hook attended to Susan's honey-do list, so he looked forward to Sunday in the lab. In the morning, however, he took his wife to her church service. He was a mostly non-practicing Catholic, and she was Evangelical and religious in her faith. During her Sunday services, his mind was usually wrapped around scientific data and scheming future research projects. He couldn't help the way his mind was wired, it was no different from when he was in Southeast Asia and contemplating the next strike against the enemy.

He dropped Susan back home, put food down for Bentley, and headed back out in the sunshiny day to the medical campus. Rarely did he work into the night hours like he'd done on Friday night, and rarely did he come in over the weekend. But he could get used to the quiet permeating the lobbies and the hallways.

Unfortunately, however, the Campus Coffee and Bakery Shop was closed, so he slipped into the cafeteria and bought a weak-looking cup of coffee and scrambled eggs in a container. Upstairs, he let his items sit while he revved up his Illumina machine to test Ms. Sisko's, or Belinda's, DNA sequences.

With the testing in progress, he sprinkled a package of salt on his eggs, a package of sugar in his coffee, and sat at his desk. He went through emails when he was finished, and went on to further comprehensive testing with the DNA Microarray to check for deletions and duplications in the sequences.

The hours ticked by, and Hook had no choice but to hit the cafeteria once again—this time for a late lunch with the only thing that resembled nutrition. He assembled a salad and lumped grated cheddar cheese and guacamole on top.

Dr. Hookie expected certain results. In the new, modern world of high-tech inventions and crime-solving methods, he believed that nothing was 'virtually impossible' to detect or discover like Kent Wadsworth had said.

It came at 5 p.m. His eureka moment! His results triumphant for his presumed hypothesis.

Several days ago, Hook had made a hypothesis. He had harbored an assumption, made before doing his DNA analysis. Now he had his theory—which was his principle about Belinda—which, along with other backing, pointed to her as the culprit!

CHAPTER 19

Monday morning Hook sneaked out of the house extra early and threw the light switch on in the lab before Cynthia and Alex. He gathered Belinda's information from over the weekend and printed out a formal detailed report for a total of nine pages.

At eight o'clock, as the lab came alive with his colleagues, he held Belinda Sisko's ticket stub and picked up the office phone.

"Miss Sisko?" he asked after dialing.

"Yes. If this is a telemarketer call, give me your personal number, so I can call you back when you're still in bed."

Hook chuckled. "This is Dr. Hookie. We met on Friday. Can you come in this morning so that we may discuss the results of your genetic analysis? I have a 10 o'clock availability."

"Oh," she stammered. "I never expected …" She put her cell phone on speaker and glanced at the clock on the nightstand. "Sure. I slept in, but I'll be there."

"Don't you want to know where?"

"Your office?"

"Yes."

"Like I said, I'll be there." She hung up.

Cynthia stood in the doorway and Hook shook his head. "Of course she knows where to be because she's been here."

"What are you talking about, Dr. Hookie?"

"That woman we met on Friday. I may ask for your help later, and it may seem odd…"

"No problem."

"That woman will be here at 10 o'clock. And tell Alex we'll be having our meeting after that."

Cynthia turned, Hook sat back down, and he scrolled through his cell phone numbers, but used his land line.

"Sydney," he said. "How about showing up in my lab office at eleven this morning?"

"Straight to the point, Hook. Good morning."

"I've never been one for lengthy small talk when directness is more to the point."

"Ha, ha. I'll remember that. Are you calling the others?"

"Right now." He hung up and dialed the extension for Kent Wadsworth.

"Kent, it's Hook Hookie."

"Hook, I believe our health fair went staggeringly well!"

"I agree. Congratulations. Can you be in my office at eleven for a group meeting?"

"Okay."

"Can you please ask Freddie Simpson to attend, as well as the primary policeman who has worked on our campus thefts?"

"I'll get on it, Hook."

Kent hung up and stepped outside his office and nodded at the receptionist. He topped off his cup of coffee from the pot on the side table and slunk back inside behind his desk. The successful fair would be a feather in his cap in the eyes of the board of directors, and there would probably be a bump in new patients to the medical campus.

Before all his day meetings began, however, he had a stack of phone calls to return and mail to attend to, all because he'd "taken off" last Friday to oversee the hospital's table downstairs.

He started from the bottom, or the oldest, of Friday's messages, and read the caller's name before him—Rachel Foreman. His receptionist had scribbled the caller's location below it—a Chicago bank. Thinking the call was legitimate, to do with some needed business with the hospital, he dialed.

"May I speak to Rachel Foreman?" Kent asked when a female voice picked up.

"This is she." She put the phone on speaker.

"Ms. Foreman, this is Kent Wadsworth from Monument Medical Center in Atlanta. I am returning your call from last Friday."

Since midnight, rain had fallen down in the Chicago area with little abatement, and she shook out her umbrella from the walk she had just made to the post office. "Just a moment. I need to refer to a piece of paper buried on my desk."

Rachel realized she had been more careful than that, opened her top drawer, and plucked out the invoice which she had found in the bottom of the artwork's carton—for the painting she'd bought last week, which now hung in her home. Her blue-green eyes settled on the slip.

"What is this about?" Kent wanted to know.

"I bought a painting last week," she said, "from a customer in my bank. When I fully unpacked the carton, I found an invoice with your name and address on it. Or, I suppose, your place of business at Monument Medical Center, Atlanta, Georgia. Technically, I am a fraud investigator for my bank. Finding this slip makes me circumspect about the origins and history of what I purchased."

Kent's eyes bulged. He couldn't believe the woman on the other end. Monday mornings were usually luckless, if not calamitous, and here some stranger several states over was telling him she had a piece of the hospital's stolen inventory.

"Right you are, Ms. Foreman. Several pieces of art were stolen from us last week before we had hung them in our lobby. They were landscapes or still life paintings, and painted with soft pastel colors."

She chewed down that information, and frowned. "This painting is forty-eight by thirty-six inches and, yes, the soft colors are marvelous."

"A rash of property has been stolen from our medical campus, and we have a team looking into it. This confirms our suspicions that whoever is doing this is organized, and now this—contacts in Illinois."

"First, I'll cancel my check to this thief. But, this is great because this woman is a new bank customer. I won't be divulging a bank customer's personal information to tell you her identity since she and I dealt with each other regarding the purchase of the painting. Her name is Linda Sisko. And hold on a minute."

Rachel scrolled the bank screen in front of her and found Linda's address, but went to the online white pages and confirmed it. "From Chicago's white pages, here's her address, which is correct." She rattled off the address. "I can contact the police."

"Hold up on doing that. We have a private investigator here. Let me run it by her."

"I also know an Atlanta based private investigator named Sydney Monaco. She may be able to help."

"She *is* helping. She is a friend of our main DNA scientist, and he brought her on board."

"It's a small world. Okay, get back to me."

"One of us will call today. Now all we need to do is find out who the brainchild of these crimes is in Atlanta."

Hook wondered only for a moment. What would Belinda Sisko look like when she showed up in his office in a few minutes? She was clever, so what he expected is what he got.

She sauntered into the lab, peering about, and noted Hook's open office door in the back. Cynthia and Alex minded their own business in their aisle as the visitor made her way through.

He pasted his eyes on her, noting her features—almost a carbon copy of last Friday—her reddish-brown hair soft and curly, stopping at her chin. Her glasses were in place, but she had forgotten lipstick, and he could not detect the freckles on her cheek. Her figure still stunning, her breasts were draped and outlined by a soft blouse. Over her right shoulder was slung the same sporty bag as the other day.

"Here I am!" Belinda said.

"Good morning."

Dr. Hookie walked around his desk, and pointed to a chair. "May I get you a soda?"

"No. I'm a coffee lover, not a pop drinker."

He pulled a soda out for himself, but left it unattended on the desk. "Pop? That is a Midwesterner's term for soda. Where are you from?"

"Georgia. Southern Georgia. I suppose I picked that term up from my sister who lives out that way."

He nodded, slid a folder in front of him, and opened it to her DNA analysis results. "I could have sworn you wore freckles the other day." He laughed, as if acknowledging a man's stupidity at wrongly noting a woman's features.

Her hand darted to her cheek. "Depends on the foundation makeup I apply. Sometimes I let my freckles shine like twinkly stars in a moonlit sky, and other times I camouflage them to hide behind the sun."

"Sounds complicated."

"Not really," she shrugged.

He popped the tab on the can. "I personally ran your analysis over the weekend."

A tendon in her neck twitched. The poor fool had spent part of his personal weekend time on her, and she was the one responsible for his recent laboratory dilemma. She wanted to feel sorry for the old man, but thought better of it.

"So what did you find? Anything I should be concerned about?"

"I must start at the beginning, Miss Sisko." He turned a piece of paper around for her to see. "This is a list of thirty genes that I can test for in my lab. I analyzed these, considered the most important." He slid a yellow highlighter down the first nine which were named: BRCA1, BRCA2, ATM, CDH1, CHEK2, PALB2, PTEN, TP53, and STK11.

"I did not ask you last Friday. Have you ever had a genetic analysis performed before? Perhaps this information is redundant to you."

"No, never." She narrowed her eyes at the sheet.

"There is bad news. You tested positive, Miss Sisko, meaning that you carry positive gene mutations." He let the information hang in the air. Although she seemed concerned, she was not taken aback.

Her finger landed on the sheet. "To all of these?"

"No." He pointed to the first two. "BRCA1 and BRCA2. Unfortunately, they are nasty little pieces of jewelry, I mean DNA chains, to succumb to gene mutations. And this is why…"

He slid out another sheet, a well laid-out graph. The top read "Lifetime Breast Cancer Risks by BRCAplus Gene (%)."

"See here the percentage risk of acquiring breast cancer with these different gene mutations, as well as the risk in the general female population, but BRCA1 and 2 are exceptionally high—with a lifetime risk of between forty-five and eighty-seven percent. This is what *you* are dealing with. As a matter of fact, not only is your chance high of acquiring a single breast cancer, but it's also above average for a contralateral breast cancer."

Hook detected a slight smile under the missing lipstick.

"Miss Sisko, it is imperative that I enlighten you about what to do with this information. I will send your reports to your obstetrician/gynecologist so that she or he orders more frequent mammograms, and you may want to consider prophylactic mastectomies, or at least speak to the recommended surgeon in this hospital."

"Too bad I didn't do genetic testing years ago."

Belinda bit her tongue, but made a decision all at once. She needed to divulge her medical history. The old scientist would find out anyway since he was sending her report to her OB/GYN doctor. In addition, she thought, now she was less vulnerable to being caught as the campus thief. As head of her "team," she had decided not to steal much more from the Monument Medical Center because their security had probably been ramped up, especially after the art thefts. The group had gained much experience, and she wanted them to move onto other medical inventory somewhere else.

Hook took a sip of soda, but studied her face. "Why?" he finally asked. "If you had done testing years ago, and learned of your significant risk for breast cancer, would you have considered a prophylactic mastectomy or a double mastectomy at that time?"

"Possibly. However, this is all a moot point. You offered me a free genetic analysis, and I was curious to see if I had inherited crappy DNA from my forefathers. I was also interested in knowing about my risk for other cancers.

"In other words, your analysis is right on the money. I was diagnosed with breast cancer a year and a half ago, and only six months ago did I finish treatment. My cancer wasn't from bad luck, or environmental, or any of the other made-up causes the health care professionals suggest to women, but from these broken BRCA genes you discovered." She thumped her finger on the sheet.

Hook felt a wave of relief course through his body. Although Belinda didn't know it yet, she had nowhere to go now but down.

"I'm sorry to hear it. Then you've been through the wringer. Did you opt for a lumpectomy, a mastectomy, or a double mastectomy?"

She laughed. "I'm a smart woman, and I did not have the benefit of today's information about a double breast risk. Anyway, I had a double mastectomy."

But he knew that. He didn't mean to, but his eyes swept over her chest, and she didn't fail to notice.

"Oh, these?!" She glanced down at her blouse. "No, I didn't have my breasts surgically reconstructed. No way. The selection of imitation gel breasts are incredibly real, along with the bras that they slip into. Patients can pick the size they want, and health insurance even helps pay for it."

"Really?"

"Yes, because it has to do with a woman's posture as well as her mental state of mind."

"So insurance paid for yours?"

"Some of it. But I have more than one set, so I pay quite a bit out-of-pocket."

"By different sets, you mean different sizes?"

"Absolutely. Actually, different cup sizes are quite fun. Like a perk after the living hell I went through for a year—chemotherapy, hospitalizations, surgeries, blood transfusions, and taste buds which made everything I put into my mouth no different from cow manure. Now, not only can I enhance my figure, but there's more."

She was on a roll, so he repeated what he said a minute ago. "For real? More what?"

Her face brightened even more. "Chemotherapy kills hair follicles, so I went bald. Never in a million years did I know about the quality or quantity of gorgeous wigs out there available to women—short, long, red, blonde, brown, black, curly, wavy, straight. There are even hairpieces that provide hair below stylish hats. Point is, variety is the spice of life, and I love living."

"But your chemotherapy is finished. Didn't your hair grow back?"

"It started to, but what the heck. I shave off what grows in, and continue to wear my wigs."

"Makes sense, especially since you must own an assortment."

She smiled, proud as a peacock, and felt smug to divulge her personal beautification methods to some old, almost-retired, man with a limp.

CHAPTER 20

With the discussion of Belinda's breast cancer over, Dr. Hookie informed her of her other risks due to her BRCA gene mutations.

"You must still remain vigilant with your health. People don't realize that it is possible to get more than one cancer. You also have a higher risk than the general population of getting ovarian, pancreatic, or malignant melanoma skin cancer. It would be wise to make an appointment with a dermatologist, and I can forward your results to them. Why don't I call the doctor at our facility and set you up? Are you familiar with our medical center, or did all your testing and treatments occur somewhere else?"

Belinda nodded. "I would like a skin doctor here. And in answer to your second question, everything I went through with my diagnosis and treatment has been here. I am so familiar with this medical center, I could draw you a map of it in my sleep."

"No need to waste your beauty sleep on cartography." He focused on his desk. "I also need to make a copy of what's in my folder for you. Why don't you go grab a bite in the cafeteria, my treat, while I accomplish this? Cynthia, my lab assistant, can go with you."

"I suppose so. An early lunch would be appreciated."

"One more thing. Maybe you can do me a favor..."

He was doing a lot to help her, she thought, so she could afford a trace of gratitude towards him. "What kind of favor?"

"There are medical privacy laws, but may I use your name? In other words, sometimes explaining breast cancer and genetic mutation research serves different purposes. It can help people." But he didn't say which people.

She shrugged. "I suppose. Sure, no problem."

Hook rose and they went into the lab.

"Cynthia, I need to prepare a file for Miss Sisko to take with her, and also make an appointment for her. I'll treat you both to a late breakfast." He pulled out his wallet followed by a bill, and handed it to her.

Cynthia stepped away from the notebook on the counter. "I would enjoy the break. Nice to see you again, Miss Sisko."

Hook made a gesture with his head. "I'll text you when I'm ready."

Cynthia gave him a thumb up—which Belinda did not notice.

Monument Medical Center was one of Sydney Monaco's favorite places to visit. Being around the campus brought back her own medical training and, although she had chosen a different path later on, she still loved to be around people who practice medicine and work in research. It was a different world, one in which she still really belonged, and respected.

She rode the elevator with an untouched cup of coffee in her hand, walked the hallway, and strode into Hook's lab.

"First one here?" she asked him. But Alex left his project and also walked into Hook's office behind her.

"Yes, have a seat," Hook waved.

Freddie Simpson slipped in, the fraction of a mustache on his upper lip flat as a pancake.

"Good morning," Hook said. "Did you use the ironing board this weekend?"

Freddie laughed. "You noticed. My work uniform is presentable on Monday mornings. It goes downhill after then."

"Perhaps you should wash it again midweek," Alex said.

"Better yet, the hospital should dry clean it for me."

They heard him before they saw him. A police officer rounded the corner and nodded at everyone. "I'm one of the policemen on your case. I don't think I met everyone before. I'm Officer Patrick."

Having met him before, Hook again shook his firm hand. Patrick took a spot against the shelves with pictures and certificates.

"One more person is needed, and then we can start. Time is of the essence." Hook rose from the sill. "Someone you all will be interested in is waiting in the wind."

Decked out in casual business attire and holding a piece of paper, Kent Wadsworth hurried into Hook's office like a desert dust ball was on his heels. "I have tremendous news," he blurted out.

Everyone stared at him as he launched ahead without interruption. "I just talked to a fraud investigator, a banker in Chicago—some woman named Rachel Foreman. She bought one of the hospital's stolen paintings from a woman customer who accidentally left the original invoice in the box. Being suspicious about the medical campus's address on it, Ms. Foreman called me last Friday. After I returned her call this morning, she even gave me the seller's name and address!"

Smiles erupted around the room as Officer Patrick took out a notepad and pen. Kent raised the piece of paper in his hand and read, "Linda Sisko."

Hook's heart thumped against his chest. "Sisko, as in S I S K O?" he spelled.

All eyes went to the scientist.

Kent nodded. "Yes, that's what Ms. Foreman said. First name Linda."

"Ladies and gentlemen," Hook went on. "I think what we have here is a family affair."

Now it was the Officer's turn to butt in. "Let me copy her address."

"Me too," Sydney added.

With their heads bent over Hook's desk, they copied Kent's note.

"But let's hear it," Sydney said.

Hook perched himself again on the window sill, satisfied that they were all ears. "I'm ninety-nine percent sure we've found our larcenist."

Alex coughed. "You mean *you* found him."

"As you young people would say, well, whatever... However, 'he' is a 'her.'"

"What have you discovered, Hook?" Sydney asked, her tone quizzical.

"I'll start at the beginning, but several things came together all at once, like a jigsaw puzzle. We all looked at camera security footage together. My lab tech, Cynthia, not only commented that someone on the videos had a walk like her pigeon-toed sister, but she also made reference in the last week about stumbling across people on campus with such a gait.

"When the 'baby at door' event occurred, my second NGS machine was stolen from the back loading dock area and Freddie spoke with a woman outside the ER—to ask her if she'd seen anything suspicious. Blonde, with shoulder-length hair, and a fine figure, the woman had that exact walk when she moved away, after they talked. However, the weird thing, when I restudied the footage, was that her hand flung up to her head—or her hair—when Freddie stepped out the automatic doors and bumped into her. I wondered why she did that.

"That woman was near the scene of the crime. I believe she was working with someone else. Next definitive thing that occurred was when my replacement NGS machine was delivered last week at the front entrance of the hospital. The same-gaited person passed us through the front door when the paintings were snatched right under our nose. Or you could say, we helped her out with them on our buggy. That person impersonated Bruce, work clothes, baseball cap, and all, and is also seen on camera."

"But," Officer Patrick said, "if you're saying it was the same person outside the ER, it's not easy for a woman to impersonate a man. I'm just saying…"

"Yes, especially since the man I passed through the automatic doors was absolutely flat-chested."

Hook pushed off the sill and grabbed a small gulp of soda.

Sydney made a counter-clockwise wave with her hand. "Go back a minute. What's your theory about said woman putting her hands up to her hair outside the ER?"

"She made that reflex because she was worried about her wig being jostled when Freddie bumped into her."

"Wig?" Sydney questioned. "So she's a master of disguise?"

"Dr. Hookie," Kent interrupted, "she can't undo her figure and end up looking flat-chested like Bruce."

"Anyone would think that," Hook agreed, "but she wears, or doesn't wear, double post-mastectomy silicone breast forms. For those who don't know about such things, they are inserted inside specially made bras. She's as flat chested as Bruce."

"Hot damn," Freddie mumbled.

"Wait a minute," Kent said, "how can you possibly know, or assume, this?"

Alex chuckled. "Never underestimate Dr. Hookie."

"The clues I mentioned were there, and I believed our thief must be very familiar with our campus. I wondered if she was a regular patient or a worker. When I started wondering about the disguises, and the possibility of false or flat breasts, the only type of person who fit that description was a male, or a woman who very likely was a breast cancer patient. Keying in on the person's gait, I watched and waited for someone fitting that description to show up at the health fair. If I could finagle it, I wanted to run a DNA analysis if it was a woman. I counted on the results showing a high probability of a breast cancer risk. If positive for certain mutations, her genetic makeup would ramp up my assumption that she was a patient here and had underwent a double mastectomy."

"So that is why you set up a second, free DNA analysis last Friday," Alex said, "in case you or Cynthia spotted a pigeon-toed female customer. You wanted to test her."

"Exactly. She agreed to the free sampling, and I performed my analysis over the weekend. Turns out she has the biggest genetic defect attributed to breast cancer, called BRCA mutations, as well as the highest chance of a second breast cancer."

With no one moving in the room, all eyes stared at Hook.

"I called her in this morning to discuss her results. Long story short, we ended up talking about, yes, her history of breast cancer, and her double mastectomies, and how she's continued to wear wigs after her chemotherapy, and even her breast bra fillers. She spilled forth the information like spilling out tokens from a winning slot machine."

"Sounds like you pinpointed our subject." Sydney laughed. "I wouldn't be surprised if you extracted a confession from her."

"He practically did," the officer said. "Are you able to tell us her name?"

"Yes. Technically, I worked that out as well. In an overall generic sense, she even gave me permission to use her name. It's Belinda Sisko. Like Linda Sisko—whom Kent just mentioned—it's S I S K O."

Officer Patrick rubbed his chin. "Sounds like entrepreneurial siblings to me. A Sisko in Chicago selling your painting, and a Sisko in Atlanta who supplied the painting."

Sydney frowned. "I bet there is more than one person involved as well."

Patrick shifted his weight from one leg to the other. "Bet we'll solve that right quick."

"I wouldn't mind looking at the security footage again," Freddie nodded.

"In lieu of spending more time on that right now," Hook said, "Sydney and Officer Patrick may want to go fetch the suspect. I've planted her in the cafeteria by bribing her to stay for a free lunch while I make copies of her DNA analysis reports. Cynthia is babysitting her."

The officer's jaw dropped, and Sydney smiled. Kent wiped his brow, and Freddie felt left out.

"Cynthia's my girlfriend," Alex said. "She's not only smart with lab research, but she's an amateur helpful detective as well."

Kent smiled. "Maybe she should get a raise."

"Dr. Hookie too." Sydney waved towards the door. "Let's go, Officer Patrick. There's someone we should meet in the cafeteria."

"I'll go too." Hook grasped the folder with the necessary brochure and copies of Belinda's result. "After all, I do owe her these genetic results."

"I'm tagging along too." Alex pushed away from the wall. "I'll lure Cynthia away from that scoundrel."

Freddie shrugged. "Y'all can't make me go away either. I want to see this woman who dressed up as Bruce."

CHAPTER 21

Trudging slowly, Hook eyeballed the entire cafeteria from the hot food area where a woman was removing aluminum containers of leftover scrambled eggs and piles of greasy sausage and bacon. The room was sparsely inhabited, which made him feel more comfortable about what was about to happen. Plus, Cynthia had made a wise choice in the seating arrangement, because both women were in the back corner near the window.

For a moment, the group of five paused and clustered together.

"They are over there," Hook motioned, "back rear."

Officer Patrick made eye contact. "You go first."

"Certainly." Dr. Hookie raised Belinda's folder near his chest.

"Alex can lure Cynthia away from the table and then Sydney Monaco and I can call the shots." Patrick put his palm out, cluing Sydney, Freddie, and Alex to single file behind him. Hook started down between a row of white cafeteria tables.

Cynthia had a visual of the approaching group and, even better, was the fact that Belinda sat opposite her.

Hook faked a smile as he handed Belinda the DNA reports he promised her.

Her eyes went from his expression, to the tan folder, to the entourage behind him. Her posture straightened and a nervous twitch crossed along her cheek. "Thank you for the information, Dr. Hookie, and the early lunch." She stood. "Nice chatting with you, Cynthia. I best be going and let your group conduct business."

As she stood, she eyed Freddie, who was giving her an up and down glance. She turned abruptly.

"It would be better for all concerned if you joined us, Miss Sisko." Sydney pointed back down to the chair, but Belinda stayed upright.

Belinda had a bad feeling about this. Only because there was a man in blue did she stay put. She narrowed her eyes and thought of the conversation she'd just had with Hook upstairs. But the old man couldn't have tied any of what she had told him, she thought, to the stolen goods disappearing from the medical center.

"Our security room has visual data that places you in a precarious position," the officer said. "First, a couple of EKG machines went missing, and then a laptop computer. Next, Dr. Hookie had the misfortune of having several genetic testing machines disappear. And then, lo and behold, artwork walked out the front entrance of the hospital!"

Belinda's scrambled eggs rose in her throat, and she fought to remain expressionless. Six sets of accusatory eyes glared at her, however, and the only way she endured them was with clenched teeth.

"I don't know what you are insinuating. Sorry I can't help you out." Her right foot toed out for a change, directed at leaving.

Sydney moved only inches, blocking her path. "Miss Sisko, your master plan, your technique of thievery, has been uncovered—thanks to Dr. Hookie."

A glazed look covered her eyes. It went away, replaced by anger. "No way. My medical history is my own."

Hook cleared his throat. "Miss Sisko, you were dealt a near-death sentence, and you were cured by medical science. And what did you do with that new lease on life but inflict harm and injustice on the very establishment that saved you? You are despicable."

With one blink of her eyes, she shrugged off his words. "You all can't prove anything."

Officer Patrick gambled next. "Your little team of coworkers are in trouble too."

Sensing total discovery, she said, "It was all the neck-tattooed guy's idea anyway."

"The neck-tattooed guy always buying coffee in the coffee shop?"

"Duane? Of course!"

"What is Duane's last name anyway?"

"Harper. I only followed his orders, or he would have hurt me."

"Really?" Sydney commented. "What about your cohorts in Chicago, even a family member?"

Belinda's shoulders sagged. They had discovered everything, and she had no idea how. "Leave my twin out of this."

Hook glanced at Kent and they smiled.

"Let's go, Miss Sisko." Officer Patrick stepped aside and tapped her upper arm.

Belinda gave Hook a last penetrating glare and left with Patrick and

Sydney.

Kent focused on Hook. "The hospital is indebted to you."

"Catching her was teamwork."

"Still, if it weren't for your sharp eye and DNA analysis …"

"Come on," Hook prompted, "we all have work to do."

"I can see the resemblance," Freddie said. "Why she got away with looking like Bruce, who helped out with the fair set up, by not wearing her false breasts."

"However, sometimes thieves overlook detail," Hook added. "It's what gets them into trouble. She forgot that she walks funny."

Sydney and Officer Patrick stood on the side of the room pouring muddy coffee into two mugs while Belinda sat on a chair alongside Patrick's desk. She faced the other way, and saw another officer escort Duane into the precinct after his assignment to go pick the man up.

The policeman walked Duane to Patrick's desk. "Wait here. The officer in charge will be over in a minute."

After dropping his jaw, Duane stood inches from Belinda's knees. The officer walked away with a nod over to Patrick.

"So *you're* here," Duane said. "That means you were caught and ratted on me!"

Sydney overheard part of Duane's barrage of words and moved closer without Patrick. Without a uniform, she figured she could easily eavesdrop.

Belinda grimaced and Duane went on. "So you think you're so smart, but here you are! Now what do you think about women running the show?"

Sydney snickered, Patrick joined her, and they went to his desk.

"Ahh," Patrick said. "Nice to meet you, Mr. Harper. Nice tattoo. I might as well tell you both together that they are picking up Linda Sisko in Chicago as we speak."

"What does she have to do with anything?" Duane asked.

"She left a Monument Medical Center invoice for the painting she acquired from you two idiots in the carton it came in…which went to the buyer."

"And you accused me of being stupid!" Duane's voice rose at Belinda.

"Which means you should've taken that out before the artwork went to Chicago."

"What are *you* talking about, Duane? You drove it there, so you should have removed any paperwork."

"You're a big dumb idiot who's dumb," he retorted.

Patrick slid a toothpick between two teeth and enjoyed the show. The two scathing lovebirds finally stopped. "Sydney, I think we have a wrap here, unless Belinda's twin sister in Chicago also had an accomplice in crime."

Belinda rolled her eyes.

Duane frowned. "Maybe you'll give me a free pass if I cooperate," he said quickly. "His name is Dirk Crouch."

"Come on," Patrick said. "Unless someone is going to post bond for either of you, enjoy your cell time." He turned to Sydney. "Thanks for your help."

"Anytime. It was fun." She pushed open the precinct door and dialed Hook.

"It's done. The Sisko sisters' endeavors are over in Atlanta and Chicago, along with their two male helpers. Belinda Sisko is going to spend part of her post-cancer survivorship years behind bars—not a pleasant way to use her 'second chance' at life."

Hook's cell phone sat next to him on the counter as the centrifuge whirled and a tube of saliva rested upright in a plastic holder nearby. Sydney's call was on speaker.

"No, it isn't," he said. "Every day of a person's first or second chance at life is a blessing in disguise. A fraction or a part of everyone's day should be spent in the interest of others or the natural world, not on something like she did to our medical campus."

At the end of the day, Hook turned the door handle and entered the house. Sitting upright, Bentley blocked his path in the hallway, insisting on acknowledgment.

"Hello, boy. Where's Susan?"

"I'm in here," Hook heard. He peeked into the laundry room where Susan held a blouse and a hanger. "I'm just finishing up a load of wash."

"I'll carry that pile back to the bedroom." He first bent down and rustled Bentley's head and then kissed his wife on the cheek. With a stack of folded clothes, he walked to the back and put away their things. When he finished, Susan handed him two hangers with tops, and he hung them in the closet.

"How was your day, honey?" he asked as they walked to the kitchen.

"Oh, the usual. I talked to the mailman for a bit, and his daughter is getting married, and our electric bill was the lowest it's been in months. Bentley went missing out back for two hours and scared the life out of me when he came back with a dead thing. Maybe a baby rabbit. I couldn't tell."

Hook poured a glass of water from the dispenser on the freezer door and scowled at Bentley. "Cats will be cats."

Susan nodded and reached for a cup. "How was your day?"

"Typical, except that the persons responsible for stealing things at the medical center are in custody."

"That's nice. I'm sure you'll rest easier." She also poured water, which Hook appreciated her drinking much more than diet soda.

"Yes. I'll be able to concentrate on my work much better now. So, what shall we eat for dinner?"

The End

FROM THE AUTHOR

If you'd like a release alert for when Barbara Ebel has new books available, sign up at: http://eepurl.com/cKrn0D This is intended only to let you know about new releases as soon as they are out.

Barbara Ebel is a physician and an author. Since she practiced anesthesia, she brings credibility to the medical background of her plots. She lives with her husband and pets in a wildlife corridor in Tennessee but has lived up and down the East Coast.

Visit or contact her at her website: http://barbaraebel.weebly.com

The following books are also written by Dr. Barbara and are available as paperbacks and eBooks:

The Outlander Physician Series:

Corruption in the O.R.: A Medical Thriller (The Outlander Physician Series: Book 1)

Wretched Results: A Medical Thriller (The Outlander Physician Series: Book 2)

The Dr. Danny Tilson Series:

Operation Neurosurgeon (A Dr. Danny Tilson Novel: Book 1).

Silent Fear: a Medical Mystery (A Dr. Danny Tilson Novel: Book 2). Also an Audiobook.

Collateral Circulation: a Medical Mystery (A Dr. Danny Tilson Novel: Book 3). Also an Audiobook.

Secondary Impact (A Dr. Danny Tilson Novel: Book 4).

The Dr. Annabel Tilson Series:

DEAD STILL: A Medical Thriller (Dr. Annabel Tilson Novels Book 1)

DEADLY DELUSIONS: A Medical Thriller (Dr. Annabel Tilson Novels Book 2)

DESPERATE TO DIE: A Medical Thriller (Dr. Annabel Tilson Novels Book 3)

DEATH GRIP: A Medical Thriller (Dr. Annabel Tilson Novels Book 4)

DOWNRIGHT DEAD: A Medical Thriller (Dr. Annabel Tilson Novels Book 5)

DANGEROUS DOCTOR: A Medical Thriller (Dr. Annabel Tilson Novels Book 6)

Other Books:

Outcome, A Novel

Younger Next Decade: *After Fifty, the Transitional Decade, and What You Need to Know.* (nonfiction health book).

EBook Box Sets:

The Dr. Annabel Tilson Novels Box Set:
Books 1-3 (The Dr. Annabel Tilson Series)

The Dr. Annabel Tilson Novels Box Set:
Books 4-6 (The Dr. Annabel Tilson Series)

The Dr. Danny Tilson Novels Box Set:
Books 1-4 (The Dr. Danny Tilson Series)

The Chester the Chesapeake Series:

A children's book series about Dr. Barbara's loveable therapy dog; illustrated with real pictures.

Chester the Chesapeake Book One
Chester the Chesapeake Book Two: Summertime
Chester the Chesapeake Book Three: Wintertime
Chester the Chesapeake Book Four: My Brother Buck
Chester the Chesapeake Book Five: The Three Dogs of Christmas

www.ingramcontent.com/pod-product-compliance
Lightning Source LLC
Chambersburg PA
CBHW021919170626
46807CB00007B/2890